Smith

LAURA LEONORA'S FIRST AMENDMENT

LAURA LEONORA'S FIRST AMENDMENT

Miriam Cohen

LODESTAR BOOKS   DUTTON   NEW YORK

Copyright ©1990 by Miriam Cohen

Library of Congress Cataloging-in-Publication Data

Cohen, Miriam.
  Laura Leonora's first amendment / Miriam Cohen.
    p. cm.
  Summary: Seventh-grader Laura finds that she must determine what her own true beliefs are in the face of widespread community opposition to admitting a boy with AIDS to her school.
  ISBN 0-525-67317-2
  [1. Prejudices—Fiction. 2. AIDS (Disease)—Fiction. 3. Conduct of life—Fiction. 4. Schools—Fiction.] I. Title.
  PZ7.C6628Lau 1990   90-6347
  [Fic]—dc20   CIP

Published in the United States by Lodestar Books, an affiliate of Dutton Children's Books, a division of Penguin Books USA Inc.

Published simultaneously in Canada by McClelland & Stewart, Toronto.

Editor: Virginia Buckley   Designer: Stanley S. Drate
Printed in the U.S.A.
First Edition

10 9 8 7 6 5 4 3 2 1

This book is Jan Solow's. With so much love and thanks to her, and to my other wonderful editors, Virginia Buckley, and Adam, Gabriel, Jem, and Monroe Cohen.

LAURA LEONORA'S FIRST AMENDMENT

ONE

"Hi, Laura!" Jennifer squeals, and pushes me right into the person in back of me, who is—Raymond! I want to bow myself down on the floor at his feet I am so embarrassed.

"Don' worry 'bout it." he says. Raymond looks like Matt Dillon, except Raymond is blond. But he's got the same deep, serious eyebrows, and he's shy too. Of course, he does have this smile like a mischievous little boy. He's talking to me, but he slants his blue-sky eyes at Jennifer. It's only natural. She's gorgeous.

"Sorry, Laura, I didn't mean it," but the way Jennifer's laughing, you know she did. And she's gone in a swooping dash of her long black hair down the hall.

"Laura, aren't you mad at her?" Martha says. But you know, I'm not. He could have growled, "Watch out, stupid," but he said, "Don' worry 'bout it.' You can tell how *really* nice he is.

Is he going to be in *my* English class or the other one? Ooh, I'm praying it's mine! BAWWP! The bell! "See you, Martha!"

I'm very busy with my head down, checking my pens and pencils and notebook. Then, he's here! Carelessly yet elegantly, he's walking to the back where Jamal and Derek are waiting. Praises to heavens!

I start writing in my notebook, the serious black-freckles kind. Lisa's has teddy bear stickers all around her name, Lisa Spinelli, on the cover. And Denise Horowitz has a giant red ♥♥ sticker on hers. I put *English 109—MRS. COOPERSMITH—Laura Leonora Fine.*

Mrs. Coopersmith is hyperactive but nice. We had her last semester. While she's taking the roll, I sneak a look at Raymond. His ballpoint is choked in his fist, squeezing out little slanty letters. I know what they're like because of a homework assignment he once threw in the basket in fifth grade. It's saved between *Black Beauty* and *Julie of the Wolves* in the bookcase in my room. Anyhow, his letters are not *anything* like Raymond. How could somebody who looks like a knight under his football helmet do tiny, weedy writing like that?

Well, some kids are word people of which I am *definitely* one. That's why they call me Laura the word nut. Others are music and art people. And some live for gym and athletics because they are more in their bodies. Raymond is like that. My dad would have liked to be a music person, but the restaurant said, "No! You have to make a living!"

"Laura, what's this nut doin' to the othuh guy?" Lisa is looking at my CPR papers, which just dropped out of my notebook.

"That's cardiopulmonary resuscitation. It's for

saving unconscious people. Martha and me took the course."

"It looks disgustin'," Lisa says.

Martha and me felt we should be ready to resuscitate people, so we took this course given by the fire department. We've been going to the shopping mall waiting for someone to collapse, only we hope it's a fairly young person, preferably a child, and definitely *not* a teenage boy! "And please," Martha says, "let it not be a drunk, or somebody with very bad breath."

The principal is rapping on the glass pane in the door with the *New York Times*. He keeps pointing to something on the front page. It's like Mr. Bender is underwater, looking in a porthole. He's holding his breath and his hairpiece is going to float away. "Keep the noise level down, class," Mrs. Coopersmith says. "I'll be right back." She disappears out the door.

Denise takes out her comb and starts digging it through her hair. "Look out, girl! Don' be combin' you' dandruff on me," Krystal says.

Krystal is a princess of Africa. Probably her mother or her sister does all her little braids and puts in those tinkly gold beads.

In a minute Mrs. Coopersmith comes leaping back. Her hair looks like it got stirred with a ladle. Her nose is quivering like an elk's. She looks like Mr. Bender just gave her the news that Emily Dickinson died and she's going to tell us about it, but she changes her mind. "Now, everybody! Let's get started on an exciting semester. I want a personal description, including what kind of books you like,

3

who you are, what you want to be, et cetera. Yes, right now. No it can't be for homework."

Mark puts away his newspaper, the *New York Times* of course, and begins. Not a second to chew on his pencil or sigh like the rest of us. He'll be the first to hold out his paper too. "I am finished!" See?

"May I read it to the class or is this personal?" Mrs. Coopersmith asks him.

"It's not personal."

"When I was born thirteen years ago in Champaign, Illinois, I was quite advanced for a child. I immediately spoke in whole sentences, and I learned to read about age three.

"I don't think you mean you were speaking when you were born, do you Mark?" Mrs. Coopersmith smiles.

"Well, no." He worms around in his seat. "I have read hundreds of scientific periodicals, as well as one hundred and five science fiction novels and I will be going to the High School for the Gifted and Talented in the Sciences, after I pass the test this spring . . ."

"Wah, wah, wah," I say, just with my lips. Hector grins and shows me the *Daily News* he's reading under his desk. "Da' Fat Boys." He points at a picture of some big, chubby boys, jumping around and singing.

"Laura?"

"Uh . . . I'm still writing."

"Krystal?"

"I don't know what we're s'posed to do."

"Well, what kind of a person are you, Krystal? Do you like mysteries, adventures, romances? I'm *sure*

4

you like romances. Have you read, *Just Say You Love Me, Stupid!* by Marjorie Reynolds Gross? Write how you feel about your life, what your hobbies are, your wishes and dreams." Krystal starts playing with the beads in her braids.

Good luck, Mrs. Coopersmith. Imagine a princess of Africa writing about her hobbies!

Denise is writing. She holds out her paper and Mrs. Coopersmith says, "Why don't you read it, Denise?"

"I like mysteries, aventures, romances and stories. My wish is if I would be sixteen. Then nobody says you can't do this. You can't do that. And my hobby and my dream is to be makeup and hair butishan."

"Good, Denise!" Mrs. Coopersmith looks at the paper, and writes *beautician* on the board.

Describe myself? I do not have a definite waistline due to the fact that my figure hasn't started yet. Also, I look too healthful, due to my mother. My hair is brown, sort of the color of an old mitten, and my head is much too small for my body. Grampa Raphael pinches my cheek and says, *shayneh maydeleh*, which means "pretty little girl," but doubtless to say, that is because he's my grandfather. Boys do *not* look around when I go by in the hall.

But sometimes I transform into Vanessa, slender girl of rich, auburn hair, trainer and rider of wild horses, bays and chestnuts and blacks. And I bring a horse to Raymond and we flow away together.

What do I want to be? Of course I don't really know yet, but

"Dr. Fine? Oh, there you are. You're so slender I didn't see you."

"Oh, please don't call me that." I chuckle. "The Dolphin Lady is what they usually call me on this Marine Biology Experimental Boat."

"Well, all right. We have a severely wounded mammal here. Is there any hope?"

"Let me examine it. There may be some hope. It's so dreadful what those nets do to the breathing potholes on these dolphins. And their whole talking system gets jiggled, sometimes permanently. See how it's unscrewed down in there? But I'll do whatever human knowledge can. This looks like a female. She's exhausted due to prostration, and her temperature is dangerously low for a dolphin. There isn't much time! She's slipping away—Godspeed, little dolphin!" I turn away to choke my sobs.

Here, on the upper deck, I can be alone. I should be used to this by now. But I'll never get used to it. I'll keep on fighting till the countries stop all cruelness to marine mammals.

I feel someone touching me sensitively on my shoulder. I turn—"Raymond! You here! I didn't know you were interested in marine biology."

"I was badly injured in football and could no longer play it," he says. "And I remembered how you got me interested in saving the air-breathing marine mammals way back in Junior High 212. And, uh—if I may say so—interested in a certain girl because she cared about the dolphins and whales."

I better get back to my real composition. "I am a twelve-year-old girl who enjoys reading. In fact, you might say that is my hobby. Some of my favorites are *Island of the Blue Dolphins, Julie of the Wolves, The Diary of a Young Girl* by Anne Frank, *The Story of My Life* by Helen Keller, and all of the Green Knowe books, especially the first one. That is where we find out that these children in the garden aren't really alive. They died in the Great Plague of about 1600. And, of course, *Black Beauty*.

"I hope we don't have to do book reports because I think that it spoils the book for you. When you are finished, you just want to think about it even when you're brushing your teeth, and riding in the car. And how can you when you are supposed to poke at it: 'What is the theme? Compare and contrast the style of this book with some other book.' Writing stories or myths are good assignments, but that is only my personal opinion." I write PERSONAL in big letters on the top, and Mrs. Coopersmith puts it on the stack.

"Thank you, Laura," she says.

She goes to the back where Raymond and all the athletic boys are leaning backward in their chairs and sprawling their legs out. Raymond and Derek and Jamal—they're too big for the seats and their hands aren't right for the books and pencils and papers either.

Raymond's handing in his paper. I hope it isn't Personal. It's not!

"I guess the most important thing in my life is sports. Especially football. I will play college football and maybe win the Heisman Trophy. I will play for five or ten years and retire and be a sports broadcaster."

It's kind of sweet the way he writes. I mean, he sounds exactly like himself. And athletes don't need to be great in English. Wouldn't that be a cute couple? Someone who's good in sports and somebody who's good in English?

Hector slides his paper to Mrs. Coopersmith. "Err, how about you reading it to us, Hector?" she says. She's having a hard time with his handwriting.

"Sure. 'Ever since I was coming here from Puerto Rico, I notice one thing. If you wanna talk about me, you talking music, man. Over on my block we got salsa, rock in roll, rappin', you name it. And sometime, me an' my frens, we went to Fat Boy concert. It were fresh! That is the best music I like.' "

"Ahhh," Mrs. Coopersmith says. Thoughts are running around like mice in her head. She wouldn't want to hurt Hector, but she doesn't know what he's saying.

She studies his paper again. "Hector, what is 'fresh'?"

"It's like cool," a bunch of kids call out.

"I had just gotten used to cool. But fresh is a colorful way to say it. Why it's fresher than cool!" Mrs. Coopersmith is really happy about her joke.

"John?" He shakes his head. John never says anything in class. He just fills up his notebook with bombs blowing up, and herds of little stick men running to a battle.

"Mark?"

Mark comes out from behind the *New York Times*.

"Would you mind telling us *what* is so interesting in the newspaper that it keeps you from participating in English 109?"

Mark starts reading, "The State Supreme Court today handed down a decision in the case of the twelve-year-old AIDS victim who is suing for the right to attend public school. The justices ruled he must be allowed to study in the same classroom as his peers.

"New York City school officials are meeting today to determine which of the city's junior high schools he will attend. That decision will be kept secret, Chancellor Brown announced, in order to prevent organized outbreaks of protest which . . ."

"There's a million junior high schools in New Yawk City," Lisa says. "He'd nevah be comin' way out heah!"

"He bettah not!" Denise starts jabbing her pen in the top of her desk.

"Ya crazy?!" says John. "My fathah'd get the whole American Legion a' Queens with M16 rifles out in front a' the school."

I'm thinking, aid means "to be of assistance, to help somebody." They *definitely* shouldn't call some awful disease by that name.

"All right, all right, people!" Mrs. Coopersmith holds up her hand. "We will not discuss it now. Henry Chen, are you ready to read your mini-auto-biography?"

Henry smiles. " 'The Return of the Star Swarm': Captain Arcturus' grim eyes focused on the galactic messenger. 'Your planetary capital will soon be destroyed, Captain Arcturus. My master, Glackto of the Urdic People, has at this moment a deadly beam of poison light on you which if it just touches a person, will kill you instantly!' The Children of Light began to wail and also, crystal tears were coming out of their electric eyes."

"Henry, that is a very exciting story. But it's not what I asked for, is it?"

Mark hisses like a sickly serpent, loud enough for the whole class to hear. " 'Crystal tears'! That's in Rol Hebert's sci-fi story 'Night on Pluto'!"

"Don' listen to him, Henry, it's good." Hector hooks a thumb at Mark. "Can ya believe this guy?"

"Lisa?"

Lisa pushes this big tree of hair away from her face. Usually she keeps it hanging down so no teacher can spy into her life. She quirks her mouth on one side. You just know she's saying "Bor-ing" in her mind.

Mrs. Coopersmith notices her watch. "My goodness, the period is almost over! But we have enough time for a little dessert, an Emily Dickinson poem about this very season." Groans from the athletes' seats. Denise and Lisa begin to file their nails.

Mrs. Coopersmith holds her book out in front like she was going to sing in the opera:

> "The morns are meeker than they were,
> The nuts are getting brown;
> The berry's cheek is plumper,
> The rose is out of town.
>
> The maple wears a gayer scarf,
> The field a scarlet gown.
> Lest I should be old-fashioned,
> I'll put a trinket on."

"Lisa, what is a trinket?"

"It's like—some kind of joolery?"

"Yes, good!"

"What do you think it means when she says, 'The rose is out of town,' Hector?"

"I don' know. Maybe the rose hangs out ovuh in Jersey."

Everybody starts laughing and slapping the desks. Hector is grinning. He knew the kids would like that.

BAWWP!

"Just a minute, class! Homework! Bring in a favorite book or poem and be prepared to discuss it orally or in writing!"

I'm standing watching Raymond going down the hall. Even his back is handsome.

"Laura? Laura! Do you feel sick?" Martha's eyes, big and brown and kind, like a pony's, are staring at me through her glasses.

TWO

Hall. For most kids this is the real, important part of school. Everybody's happy banging their lockers, swirling their hair with a brush from their pocket-books, and searching with their eyes for "certain persons." Like Martha for Ricky.

I can tell you true scientific facts about this junior high. It's two flavors of Jell-O in those tall, curvy glasses. The top is red raspberry, like rubies, and the melty clouds of whip cream just drip down on it. Helene, Zoe, Alec, Jeff, and Raymond are raspberry, of course. They have this easy style and deep auburn or champagne-blond hair. I don't know if they are, they just look richer. But Raymond is different. Even though he's so tan and perfect, inside he's really shy.

OK. The lime-green bottom flavor is me and most of the rest of the school. But I believe it *could* happen that a raspberry boy could go with a lime girl, if she is a good person that has interesting thoughts. Of course, she has to have normal attraction.

Martha leans over my shoulder to put her jacket

away. She shares my locker. "What did you bring for your favorite book?" She has English 109, the other section.

"*You* know, Martha."

"Not again!"

"Yep." I hurry away to Room 109, plump into my seat, and flip open my paperback copy. It had to be *Island of the Blue Dolphins*, because every time I read it, I cry. How could this girl, Karana, have such courage? I like to think about people that have courage, I don't know why. But I always worry that *I* might not have it, courage, I mean.

Danny is telling something to Mark. Their eyeglasses nervously twink at each other. "They don't know! They don't know how this AIDS virus operates! They can't be sure!"

"Some scientists have traced it to Africa, eating green monkeys or something."

"But I don't think they can be sure that it couldn't be transmitted by handshakes or maybe even by your breathing." Mark and Danny *like* thinking about awful things!

Mrs. Coopersmith finishes checking the roll and leaps up from behind her desk. "Danny, what is your choice?" Danny is a grade ahead for his age, and he's all small and nervous from being so brilliant.

"His favorite is da en-cycle-pedia." The kids laugh and Hector stands up bowing and waving.

"Class! I know we all like to have fun, but"—Mrs. Coopersmith beams her glasses hard on Hector— "we don't do that here."

Danny lugs *The Complete Sherlock Holmes* out of his briefcase. "There's a part in 'Study in Scarlet' where Sherlock Holmes explains how his great brain operates." He fumbles for a while. "I can't find it, but I admire Sherlock Holmes because he uses his brain to solve a case. He doesn't just shoot his enemies with some dumb, supermagnum dagger-gun, like James Bond."

"Ooh, James Bond is *cool!*"

"His car! Man, did you see that car goin' on the water and this parachute explodes out of it when it blows up?"

"Boys!" Mrs. Coopersmith is trying her attack-chicken method again. "We are *not* discussing James Bond. Thank you, Danny."

Mrs. Coopersmith turns to find Krystal with her back to Denise, who's doing some of Krystal's little braids. "Ladies! This is not a beauty parlor! Krystal, have you done your assignment?" Krystal sways her head elegantly on her Egyptian queen neck, a "no" for Mrs. Coopersmith.

"Denise?"

"I'll bring it tomorrow. It's on the kitchen table right by the toaster. You could go there yourself if you don't believe me! I was in a hurry. I din' wanna be late, so I forgot it." Mrs. Coopersmith sighs, but she's really trying to believe Denise.

"Laura, are you prepared?" I shove my composition at her, wanting her to read it, but I'm embarrassed. It's probably too dramatic and not enough facts, which is, actually, the kind of person I am.

"Island of the Blue Dolphins. This is my favorite book. Perhaps the reason is because it is about courage. A person doesn't usually get the chance to know if they are courageous or not, the way Karana did.

"She didn't cry or scream with hysterics when the boat with everybody in her tribe sailed away. She just did all the things you do everyday, like washing the dishes (which were made of shells and stones) and building her own sort of cave house. For eighteen years (!) she stayed alone on that island with only her animals for company.

"When Karana says, 'For animals and birds are like people, too, though they do not talk the same or do the same things. Without them the earth would be an unhappy place,' I agree perfectly with her in these ideas.

"Let me see your copy, Laura." Mrs. Coopersmith opens to the part where Karana has to decide if she will kill the wild dog who tore apart and killed her little brother. Now he's at her feet, wounded by her arrow. Somehow, she can't do it. Instead, she puts Indian herbs on the dog and he becomes like her animal brother. Mrs. Coopersmith is asking, "If you were in Karana's place, would you have killed the dog?"

Mark votes "kill," and so does Raymond. I think Raymond isn't even really listening—he just wants the class to be over because P.E. is next period. But Mark *would* do it.

Hector says, "If he woulda' killed my lil' brother, I would kill duh dog. But 'den, I would be sorry."

"Ah ha!" Mrs. Coopersmith holds her finger up like an exclamation point.

"A dog jus' doin' what it have to do. Why you gon' kill it?"

Mrs. Coopersmith is almost skipping around, she is so happy that Krystal is "participating." *"Good* thinking, Krystal!"

Most of the girls vote they wouldn't kill. I think girls have rounder thoughts and boys have sharper, more killing ones.

Mrs. Coopersmith is hugging herself, she's so glad everybody is interested in the topic. "Raymond, have you anything to add to this question?" Raymond tosses the tumbling gold hair back from his eyes, which happen to be a beautiful old-blue-jean color, and shrugs. She shouldn't embarrass him! He has deep and interesting thoughts—you can see that from his eyes. But he is shy. He can't give his deepest thoughts out to just anybody. "What book did you select, Raymond?"

Hit the Line for Winbrook High! is the book Raymond holds up. "Well, uh, this book is about a guy named Randy Gibbs. And he is a freshman who is a terrific forward passer. Well, just before the big game, this guy that's jealous of Randy tells the signals to the other team. But Randy suddenly calls new signals and he's running down the field when this two hundred and eighty-five pound tackle is blocking him and three guys try to bring him down. Crunch! He breaks away and guys are smacking into each other trying to nail him. But they can't. He's in the clear and over the goal line!"

I feel it's almost like poetry, that "Crunch!"

But Hector asks, "Man, tell me somethin'. Why you wanna get ya face stepped on, an' ya kidneys busted. My girlfrens don' wanna see me all messed up when I go dancin'. I gots to look fresh for my girlfrens."

Raymond looks through him as if Hector was a speck of dirt on the window. Then Raymond says,

"*You* wouldn't understand." And Hector is grabbing Raymond's football jacket by the front. Mrs. Coopersmith pounds down the aisle, but it's too late! They're thudding their fists on each other and cursing. Lisa and Denise sit up like, "Hey, this movie's fine'ly starting!" All the air in the room is getting sucked toward Hector and Raymond, and I feel sick. It's awful and none of the kids yells "Stop!" *Please* make them stop, Mrs. Coopersmith! She is trying, but they're like strong men.

"Boys! That's enough! We don't do that here—I won't have it! I am disappointed in both of you!"

"Ayy!" John is cheering. "They got guts!"

Mrs. Coopersmith pulls Hector back to his desk, and Raymond flicks off his jacket where Hector's hands were. They're not hurt, thank goodness!

Mrs. Coopersmith sits at her desk, looking as if she wants to cry. Then she goes and stands at the board, straightens her back, sticks out her chest like she's taking the Pledge of Allegiance, and she's the captain of her boat again. "Class! Take out your notebooks. You will write on this theme." She puts on the board:

DOES IT TAKE REAL COURAGE TO FIGHT?

"Each of you will have to think of your own definition of courage—"

BAWWP!

Squeezing out the door, I'm trying to see if Raymond is really all right. Denise grabs Lisa's arm. "Did you see 'Poor Sister, Rich Sister' last night? This man pushes Melanie in front of this horse her sister's husband was riding on. But see, he didn't even know it's Melanie. He thinks it's Tiffany!"

17

Lisa is hugging her books and dipping nail polish with a little brush onto these pink spoons at the end of her fingers. Danny is shouting at Mark, "It does *so* take courage to have wars! There couldn't be history without wars!"

And Krystal says, "Don' take no courage come upside some girl's head, she be axin' for it."

Oh Raymond, with your eyes like two blue lakes by the tawny sands out west someplace. You are not a vicious person that likes to fight, even though you play football. And Hector isn't, even if his neighborhood is more tough. I don't know what to think.

THREE

The purple and red neon sign in the glowy yellow window is winking. "Come inside, where it's warm as the smell of Sarah's challah bread. You'll find beans and mushrooms, kasha and onion, so cozy together in the soup of the day. Hungarian, Russian, and Jewish East Side specialties are inviting you. Come!" The S & L is truly a Pure and Homemade Vegetarian-Dairy Restaurant. "S & L" stands for Sarah and Leonard, my mom and dad.

We wipe away the steam and look in the window. Inside is a lighted-up stage, with actors making talking motions with their hands and forks and spoons. "C'mon, Martha." I push open the door. The voices and smells grab us and bustle us right in so we are actors too.

There really isn't room for all the people and tables and food in that little restaurant. But everybody is happy to keep pushing in sideways and stand waiting for a stool or a table.

"Look who's here! It's my daughter and her little friend!" Neither Martha or me is little anymore, but that's how daddies always talk. I'm proud of mine. He's the star actor, joking and running up and down behind the counter, frying potato pancakes, slapping chunks of buttered challah on the little plate—it comes free with your soup. His worrying self he puts away when he ties on the white apron. "Customers don't come to hear *your* worries. They got plenty of their own." So he leans over the counter and says, "Meyer, when you weren't looking, I just saw Ben dip in your soup with his challah," which isn't true, but that's part of Dad's act. And this *is* such a small place, you do have to watch out—it might happen.

Mom is the orchestra conductor back in the narrow kitchen with no door. "Hello, darling! Martha! How are you? Wait, as soon as I'm not busy, I'll sit down with you for a minute." But Mom is never not busy. She is pulling the loaves of challah in their black pans out of the oven, she is checking on the tall pots bubbling like volcanoes, she is rolling a pie. Whenever I go back there, I think the stove is a huge, fat iron lady, with the kettles and cooking pots on her lap. She is steaming and humming, "Sarah! Soups, stews! Give me more! Even for tea I've got room."

"Yeah, Poppy!" That's what Ramon calls Dad: It's Spanish for father. "One health salad down here!" And Daddy makes a quick igloo out of cottage cheese, plops the Jell-O on a lettuce leaf, and skates the thick white dish down the counter where it stops in front of the right customer.

When I come in, Daddy sees me right away, no matter how busy it is. "Here's my daughter," he tells everybody. "Laura Leonora, the smartest in seventh grade junior high school. And Martha, also smart, and a terrific piano player." There's no use my telling him, "Mark is smarter, and so is Danny, and Jennifer Pascaglia is *much* better in math." But it's sweet he remembers Martha takes piano.

"She writes stories, my daughter. You ought to see how she writes stories!"

"Maybe she'll be a reporter or a journalist?"

"That's right, if somebody doesn't see her and marry her first."

"Listen, these days the girls are smarter as the boys. I got a niece is a college perfessor."

I don't really mind these embarrassing remarks—I'm used to the customers since I was a little girl. But I whisper to Martha, "They can't help it. They think they're saying praising things!"

People are sitting pressed together at the counter, but some are really sitting alone on their stools. They lean on their elbows over their dish and stare far away, doing what Grampa Raphael says you should when you eat—*"Ess un gedenk,"* which means "Eat and think." Not Martha and me. We like to eat and talk.

As soon as one of the little tables for two against the wall comes empty, we take our rice puddings and sit down.

It's relaxing, licking a spoonful of creaminess with little pebbles of rice and soft, wrinkly raisins.

"When I was younger," I tell Martha, "I used to pick out all the boiled bugs. That's what I called the raisins." We lick peacefully. "How far back can you remember, Martha?"

"Umm—I don't know."

21

"I can remember when I was two, my gramma was teaching my mom how to make rice pudding. I was kicking my legs on the kitchen chair and playing with a big spoon, and Gramma says, 'Now, you'll throw in a nice handful of raisins, a good sprinkle of cinnamon.'

"How much, Mama?' My mom's writing it down.

"Right away, you'll see,' Gramma says. 'Put down, "Plenty raisins." With the cinnamon, put, "Just a little, not too much." '

"My mom shakes her head. 'What kind of recipe is that?' "

"Laura, you mean you can remember *all* that and you were only two?"

"Well, that's how they'd always talk. Gramma used to put me on her lap, and pat my hands together, and she'd sing in her olden language, Yiddish. It was a song about a pretty little girl and some riddles, *Du Maydeleh du Shayns*. And she'd make up funny little Gramma stories so I'd stop crying. One was how Mickey Mouse was coming in his airplane to take me to Macy's department store."

"You must have liked your gramma a lot."

"Oh, yes! Probably that's why I love rice pudding. When I'm eating it, I always remember her."

Martha reads the menu that's in white letters on black over the counter.

"What's 'Vegetarian Chopped Liver,' Laura?"

"It's vegetables all chopped up to taste like liver."

"Oh. Why don't they just chop up liver?"

"They can't because it's for vegetarians: Vegetables are sort of their religion."

"You mean they worship vegetables?"

22

```
VEGETARIAN CHOPPED LIVER
•
STUFFED CABBAGE
•
HOT NOODLE PUDDING
•
GEFILTE (Chopped) FISH
•
BLINTZES
(Cherry, cheese, blueberry
all served with sour cream if desired)
```

You shouldn't laugh at anybody's religion, but that sounds so funny we can't help it. After, I tell Martha, "I first learned to read by saying our menu."

Ellen is coming out of the washroom, putting her hair spray in her handbag, and patting her huge hairstyle. It looks like it died and got stuffed and put back on her head, but I'd *never* tell her that. She's too nice. She perks her crispy white hanky in its pocket on her black uniform. "You got to look good for the customers. That the diff-ernce between a perfessional and one of those young girls with their hair flying all around," Ellen says.

"How ya doin', baby? Hi, Martha. How's school?"

I grin up at her. "Good, Ellen." Before I finish, she's whisking away to fill up a napkin holder that's empty, and handing a ketchup bottle to somebody before they even know it's not on their table. Ellen is a Manhattan person, so she's more adult than my parents. She won't get upset if I ask her something later, something bodily.

Now, I'm not saying this could ever, ever, in the wildest possibility, ever happen, but if Raymond came to our restaurant, what would he think? Would he think it was maybe people talking too much and waving their hands and stirring in their soup with their bread? He is from a different background of life, where nobody pulls in their soup with happy smacks and people don't talk loud. But, no, I just feel he wouldn't snob any person just for that. He's too nice.

"Martha, did you have enough to eat? Anything you want now? Don't be shy." Daddy sits down with an "oof" for his sunken arches that even special shoes don't fix. He pulls the glass sugar shaker toward him and sprays it into his coffee like he's watering a lawn.

"Daddy! If Mom sees you, she'll get upset."

"If Mom sees *what*, she'll get upset?"

"Did you have to come just now?" Daddy says to Mom, who is stealing a minute for a cup of coffee too. Only she breaks a little envelope of Sweet 'n Low in her coffee.

"Is he dumping sugar in his coffee again? Leonard, it's bad for your cholesterol, *please.*"

Dad is a good worrier, but Mom is the *Guinness Book of World Records* champion. With Mom, it hasn't happened yet, but it might: a bomb, an automobile accident in which we are *all* killed, except Mom. "I would be left all alone to suffer," she says.

"Laura, your hair looks nice today. Did you take your vitamins?"

"Mom, don't worry. I took my vitamins."

"If I didn't worry about her, how would she know I loved her, right Martha? What kind of mother would I be?" I hug her to show she's a good kind of mother, but it's hard to be the child of somebody who worries all the time. Martha doesn't know. She's got a sister to spread the worry on.

"Look at this, Len." Mr. Grossbard is leaving and he slaps down the *Daily News* in front of my father. "Did you see this? A ten-year-old kid, an only child, died from heart trouble, can you imagine? They tried to give another heart but it didn't fit, or something. No matter how long they are living, the mother and father will suffer, every day they will suffer."

Mom looks so sad, like her own heart is getting a terrible pain. "Ay! That poor mother. That is the worst, the worst that can happen to a person, to lose a child. It's all right for us older ones to go. That we expect. But a child! I pray to God for my own Laura to be well. That's all I ask from God, nothing else, only that one thing."

"I know what you mean, Mrs. Fine. It's exactly like myself. Of course, we have three, but still. It wouldn't matter how many you had. That one, that you lost, you can never get over it."

Daddy doesn't say anything. He just looks as if he's swallowed a big gray stone. I whisper to Martha, "Why do they talk about things like that all the time? Thank goodness, kids don't."

"I know," Martha whispers back.

"I mean, there are *awful* things that can happen to kids, but if you're always thinking about it, that would just make you old."

"Daddy, could Martha and me put on the radio?"

"Certainly, honey."

I put on the music station. That's what he adores. When he was growing up, they couldn't afford music lessons, so when somebody gave him an old saxophone, he played without the notes.

They go back to work and I feel a little sad. I always do when I watch them working. If I say, "Let me help. Let me do something. I could clean off the tables or chop carrots for Mom in the kitchen," the answer is, "No, darling, you study. That's your job. Here it's so small, you'd only get in the way. Have some more rice pudding."

"Martha, do you want some more rice pudding?"

"No thanks. I've got to go to the bathroom."

Ellen is walking the dishes up her arm, six of them in stacks, and grabbing the ketchup bottle and the two empty Dr. Brown's Cream Soda bottles between the fingers of her other hand. I follow Ellen to where she unloads her dirty dishes in the big plastic pan for Ramon to carry to the sink.

"What color is your nail polish, Ellen?" I'm not really interested. I just have to catch her and talk about something *very* personal. Well, it isn't personal to me as a person. I mean, *I* would never get it. And I'm sure it will get cured and we won't have to worry about it anymore. Not that I *do*. I *never* think about it because it doesn't do any good. But could my mom and dad get it? At a certain time of the month, for girls, could it find a way to go up *in* you, because there's blood? Could a whole seventh grade get it if the AIDS boy came to our school?

I take her hand and spread the fingers out so I can

pretend to admire her nails. They are orangey red and shiny like candy, with silver specks.

"This here is, let me see—I think it's Crushed Peaches in the Snow."

"How can you always keep them so nice, Ellen? Mom only uses nail polish when she goes to a wedding or bar mitzvah."

"You've got to freshen it up about every other night if you want it to look right. You thinkin' of becomin' a woman and puttin' on nail polish?"

"Ellen, I don't even wear lipstick yet! Maybe I won't ever, because sometimes they use whales to make lipstick." I'm really just trying to keep Ellen till I can say it—"Ellen, what is AIDS?"

"It's nothin' you have to worry about, honey. Kids don't do things that'll get them in . . . errr . . . *that* kind of trouble. An' *that's* a fact. I got to finish up." She's really relieved to get away and her busy nurse's shoes dash her off.

Martha's back and Ramon is calling, "Poppy, time to close. You gonna stay here all night?" Maybe they would like to, because they will just have to hurry over the bridge and hurry into Queens and hurry into bed and quickly wake up at 5:00 A.M. tomorrow to hurry over the bridge again. It's lucky Ramon helps them so much, and Ellen.

"Come In. We're Open" flips over to "Sorry, We're Closed" on the door. Ramon is turning up chairs on the tables with their legs kicking in the air, so he can swoop the mop everyplace. Ellen lets me and Martha clean the tops of the ketchups with her. "Not many people realize, if you didn't swirl the wet rag around the neck of the bottle, there'd be an ugly crust next day for the customers," I tell Martha.

Daddy has to wash and rub the metal-and-glass steam table till it shines, and tuck the tuna salad that didn't get ordered into the icebox. The soft, oval-shaped challah doughs are relaxing in their pans on the wooden table in the kitchen, waiting for Mom to pull the white cloths over their heads. Then they will sleep warmly and rise higher and rounder in their beds till it's morning.

"Good night, everybody!"

"Good night, good night."

"Take care, Mr. Fine."

"*You* take care, Ellen. And you also, Ramon."

"See you in the morning!"

"What else?"

We're in the back of our car. Daddy's head with his few hairs standing up is dark and round against the windows. The night city is twirling past. Ever since I'm a little girl playing with my dolls and animals in the backseat, I know Daddy will drive us safely to wherever we're going. "Watch this, Martha. Mom's going to turn around to check if I'm all right," I whisper. Mom looks back.

"Laura, are you all right, darling?" Martha and me giggle.

Then we lie back gazing at the million apartments, like tall books opened up, printed with words of light. The Chrysler Building is a tall gray warrior with a golden helmet, and the Empire State floats up to touch the purple sky with its needle as we are going over the bridge to Queens.

If this bridge should collapse, and our car was sliding straight toward the gulping black water way below,

what would I do?! Could I save us? Martha'd cry. Mom
would be screaming, and Daddy would be so nervous
he'd put on the gas. I'd reach for the brake and shout,
"Don't move! And whatever you do, stay calm! Remem-
ber, I can do CPR . . ."

FOUR

Up, up, up, up four flights of stairs and I'm knocking on Grampa Raphael's door. Grampa's slippers come *shoof, shoof* down the hall. "Ah ha!" His nose and beard peek around the door like Santa Claus (if there could be a Jewish Santa). His smile comes beaming out from his little eyes like Santa's too. And I am beaming back.

He leads the way down the hall and I hug the smells, the nice old smells of Grampa Raphael's apartment, into me. The worn-out brown velvet chair and sofa are part of it, the curtains thin as the air moving softly in the window, the faded rugs that know Grampa's slippers so well, and remember Gramma's. Everything together smells like somebody nice has been living here a long time.

"So, Laura Leonora, how are your momma and poppa?" My momma is Grampa Raphael's daughter, Sarah, and she is married to my dad, Leonard.

"They're good, Grampa. They sent you this." I put in his hand the white cardboard box with his favorite raisin strudel made by Mom. Now we will sit by the window at the white enamel kitchen table. A cup and saucer are waiting and a glass with Pebbles Flintstone on it. "Sit, sit, Laura," Grampa says, and brings out a little brown paper bag. I know what's in it—marshmallow bells.

"My favorite." I grin at Grampa. He will have tea and raisin strudel, while I always have milk and marshmallow bells. There is a cookie hidden on the bottom, then red jelly and a puff of white marshmallow, all covered by a chocolate skin you can crack off with your fingernail.

"The sunshine is my tablecloth. How do you like that?" Grampa pats the tabletop and smiles at me. That's what we mostly do—grin at each other—because we're a team.

The only time Grampa doesn't smile is when Mom thinks he can't take care of himself. Then he gets *furious*. All of a sudden, he looks tall like Moses, so I don't recognize him, and he shouts, "I am not going to live with anybody! I am living with myself, absolutely, one hundred percent OK! I am still a man! I didn't become a baby! Thank you very much!"

"Grampa Raphael, what do you think of football?" I'm thinking about my courage composition for Mrs. Coopersmith. I take exactly one mouthful of milk with one bite of marshmallow bell. Grampa is drinking his tea with the spoon sticking in it because that's the way his Grampa did.

"Football? I didn't think about football lately. Why?"

"I mean, do you think it takes courage to play football, *real* courage?"

Grampa shakes his head. "So much smacking and

31

knocking down. This is a game? Personally, I'm not intending to go on the Yankees."

"That's baseball," I say. "Seriously, Grampa, some boys think this is a chance to be like the heroes of olden times. And you don't get many chances to show if you have courage these days."

"Oofah!" says Grampa Raphael. "It's already ten o'clock. I've got to open up the store or Mrs. Mendelson will say I'm getting lazy."

I help him put away the few things, and while he's in the bathroom, I plump down on the sofa, which sighs, "Ay, Laura Leonora, sit quietly, please." It remembers me when I was small, jumping off its fat arms onto its brown, soft velvet belly.

"Come, Laura Leonora. There is a crowd of ladies maybe, with their shopping bags, begging to come into my store." That's a Grampa joke because Grampa spends most of his time reading behind the counter of his store—A Button for Every Purpose. It's really half a store, divided down the middle. The other side is Mrs. Mendelson's United Umbrellas. But you don't need much room to keep thousands of buttons in little drawers and trays and folded paper envelopes. No one realizes how many buttons there are in this world, Grampa says—how many there were before zippers came, that is. He says, "Clothing comes and goes, but the buttons remain."

We're going down the narrow, brown-painted hallway and stairs, with me pretending I always walk this slow. On the street, Grampa is smiling and nodding to all his friends. "You know my granddaughter? She's visiting me today."

"I didn't recognize her! I remember she was a

little tot! She's getting *so* big!" I look someplace else. It's embarrassing. I feel like that lady in the TV news that's so fat she can't get through her apartment door to go shopping.

We stop at the candy store for a paper, and next door is Grampa's button store. A lot of people are *not* waiting to get in. In fact, nobody is. But Grampa cheerfully rolls up the iron shutters, *clong, clong, clong.* With his hand he brushes away a bit of dust from the customer's chair. "Sit, Laura." I always love being here. It's such a friendly mess. Grampa bustles around, arranging boxes and trays, putting something here, something there. Then he is satisfied everything is ready.

The morning goes by with just the nice sounds of reading; me in the customer's chair with the diary of Anne Frank, which I am rereading for my English assignment, and Grampa Raphael on the stool, leaning over the *Daily News* on the counter. Every now and then he makes sounds with his tongue, "Tsa, tsa." That means, "Can you imagine?" People who jumped on the subway tracks to save another person are his favorite story. "You see," he says, "there are still plenty of good people."

There's a picture on the other page—it's this poor, collapsed horse. He's white, with a kind, sad face, and he's on the sidewalk with people throwing buckets of water on him. That's not what he needs! They made him work too hard, and they should give him a horse massage and mashed oatmeal.

Oh, it gets me so mad! That mayor, it's his job to take care of all citizens, and that includes horses.

It's Central Park by all the hotels where the horse-taxis are. I'm sitting up high on my driver's seat, flickering the whip, but not on the horse. It's just for the style, like my black high hat. I'm wearing one of those black coats, with a white scarf crushed under my neck. And whitish-tan pants puffed out on the sides like handles, and leg-high black boots. And there's the lovely horsey smell, which some people might not like, but I do. It's better than the silly perfume women smear on themselves.

My horse is the best treated of course. He's all powerful and bunchy from the good food I feed him. I personally polish him every day, and I've stuck plastic roses in his mane and around the horse-taxi roof. His name is Black Star because he's black with a white star on one of his ears.

The other drivers don't care a bit about their horses. They're sleeping or eating, just waiting to get done so they can go home. Oh yes, they care about the people who go for a ride and pay money! For money-people they're all smiley smiley. They run around and tuck them in a warm, puffy robe and bow their high hats to them.

There's this old horse, Whitey. He's tried all his life to be a good horse and do whatever his cruel master wants. Suddenly, he collapses down in the street! People are stopping to look like it was a show. "Guess he's ready for the bone factory."

I leap down from my seat. "Get back! Give him air! I'm ready to do CPR!" I kneel down and pat his head. "Take it easy, good old boy. I'm going to help you." But it's too late! He rolls his eye at me like he wants to say something, and dies in my lap.

I'm looking up with tear-soaked eyes, and just at that minute, coming out of he twirling doors of the snobbiest hotel in New York, is the mayor! I point. "Look what you have done. How would you *feel if you had to pull four, sometimes five people* and *a driver, in rain, and hail, and boiling heat? Have you ever read* Black Beauty? *Here, you may borrow my copy."*

"Oh, God! I remember now!" the mayor says. Black Beauty. *I read it when I was young. How could I have forgotten? From now on, every taxi-horse in this city will have full police protection around the clock, even in their stables."*

"Laura Leonora, are you here or did you fly away someplace like a little bird?" Grampa asks. I come back from Central Park, and I grin. I would be a pretty heavy little bird.

"Grampa Raphael, did you ever hear about this book?" I hold it up.

"Maybe I heard something a long time ago. So tell me again, what's it about?" I show him the cover. "Something with the face of that girl is like you, around the mouth."

"Oh Grampa, she died in the concentration camps and she was only fourteen. But first she had to hide for two years in this attic with her sister and her mother and father just because they were Jews! Also, there was a boy who became her friend. And they knew the Nazis could come and grab her and her family from the attic and take them away. And they did! But first, she wrote everything down in her diary. And you know, it isn't a sad diary. I would have spent all the time crying and being afraid, but she kept on chatting to her diary and trying to be a good person. She fought even though she didn't fight, somehow. Remember, I was asking you about football, Grampa?" He nods. He can listen for the longest time and never says, "Hurry up already, Laura, please!" I think even if a customer came, she would have to wait.

"What I am trying to find out is if it takes real courage to be in a football game, and know you have to attack and be attacked, and maybe be hurt badly. Football isn't exactly fighting, but it's sort of like a war."

"This I don't know, because I wasn't playing football when I was a youngster. Stickball we played, and you didn't attack nobody. I was a young man, with a family already here, not over there, when the war was going on."

"Grampa, do you know about plagues? That's when a terrible disease kills everybody?"

"Such a thing I didn't see. But when I was a boy, people called sometimes on each other a curse, a *choleriya*, which was a certain type of sickness, a cholera. And that meant, a cholera should come, like a devil, and carry you away.

"But usually, this is only if a very rich man was owning everything and squeezing the poor families. Then they'd say it, 'a *choleriya* should come for the landlord, Meyer Moskowitz,' or 'Benjamin Rothstein,' or whatever was his name."

"But I mean a *real* plague, Grampa. Like I read this book about some children that died in the Black Plague in about 1600. And I just kept saying, Why

36

did they have to die? They didn't do anything wrong or anything? Even today there are things like that. How can this just happen to people, even kids that are good?"

"This is a *very* big question, Laura. You know you're named from my sister Leonora, may she rest in peace. Well, she died with something you could say was like that. A lot of people died in those days, but, of course, not everybody. TB, that was the name of the sickness. You got it from the tenements, which was the apartments all cramped together, which didn't give enough air. So my sister started coughing, and she got thinner, and the doctor couldn't help, nothing could help. Not even if you had money. So we took turns staying with her all the time, holding her up in the bed so she could breathe better."

"Weren't you afraid to catch it?"

"Um, I don't think so. We just worried the sick person should get better.

"Ah ha! What can I do for you today, Mrs. Pintchik?" A customer!

Mrs. Pintchik holds out a piece of velvet. "Royal blue. I must have royal blue buttons to match, maybe something with a little gold. It's my daughter-in-law's hostess gown, you know, for entertaining a cocktail party. It's gorgeous, so the buttons gotta go with it perfect."

Grampa hurries around the counter. "I have something here that might be just the thing," and he reaches up high for a box with other boxes stacked on top. "Here is a very attractive button . . ." Balancing on a little stepladder, he pulls that box out and the others fall down into the space like a magic trick.

"I have here something you will *love*. A square model, just the color, plus a touch of gold."

Mrs. Pintchik makes a pickle face. "No! It's too square. What else have you got?"

Grampa comes the rest of the way down the ladder. "Let me see . . ."

Finally, Mrs. Pintchik goes away satisfied but still looking like a sour pickle. I make a face as she closes the door. "Grampa, don't you hope all the buttons pop off her daughter-in-law's gorgeous gown, and dive into her gorgeous sour cream–and–onion dip, at her gorgeous cocktail party?"

"Laura Leonora, you are a rascal!" Grampa laughs.

It's 11:45, not really lunchtime yet, since we came at 10:30. So Grampa goes back to the comics and I try working on my courage composition. I guess older Jewish people don't think football is good. It just looks like fighting to them. And it's hard for them to understand that Raymond and Derek and Jamal love to play because their bodies are really smart at this. Yes, you can be smart in your body, *not* just your brain. But younger Jewish people like me *could* see something courageous about football. And after all, Raymond might be terribly injured!

"What would you say to a hot dog with sauerkraut, and for me, onions; for you, no onions?"

"But what if we miss some customers, Grampa? I can wait."

"Well," he says, closing up the cash register, "this is the off-season for buttons, you know. After lunch we'll have more strength to work again."

Goody! Hot dogs! Your mouth starts leaking just thinking about it.

Mrs. Mendelson from United Umbrellas is standing in the doorway. "How's business, Mr. Warmbrand?"

"Getting better," Grampa says. "We're taking a little time off to go to Kazimir's for a hot dog."

"Enjoy, enjoy," Mrs. Mendelson says, and goes back to her store for another customer. Why do people need so many more umbrellas than they do buttons? It's not fair!

Sauerkraut smell snatches your nose and pulls you right into Kazimir's. The busy, steaming air even tastes like a delicatessen. Grampa told me that means "delicate eating."

It is *so* good! Grampa has knockwurst. Mine is a regular hot dog with mustard. We share French fries with plenty of ketchup, and cream soda is our wine.

Afterward, we stroll outside, calm and happy, with garlic burps to bring back the memories.

"Ah ha, there is Ramon's car in front of my stoop. You're just on the right time." He is here from Daddy's restaurant to pick me up. We hurry toward Ramon's old green Pontiac, which has the back end lifted up higher than the front. "It gives more style," he says.

Just as Grampa is shaking his hand and I am smiling "Hi," a man with his hair in ashy, dirty points all over his head comes in front of us. His bare feet are the same color as the sidewalk and his eyes are scary red.

"I got a nine-year-old kid waitin' at home, an' I jus' come out of the hospital with shingles, which is a very painful disease. I jus' need a little help gettin' back on my feet. Fifty cents, a dollar, anythin' you wanna give . . ."

39

Grampa pulls up his coat and starts searching for his little leather purse.

"Hey, Mr. Warmbrand! You don't wanna be givin' away your money like that. He jus' gonna drink it up." Ramon shakes his head while Grampa puts a dollar in the man's hand. Mumbling, he goes away, from one side of the street to the other.

"Well, maybe he does have a child at home. It's possible," Grampa Raphael says.

FIVE

Danny bumps into the door with a big cardboard box in his arms. "My history project," he tells Mark, who's giving it the needle eye. "It's a time line that tells all the things that happened in history, in recorded time, of course."

Mark's long, mosquito nose dives over the side of the box and begins sawing off bits of Danny's project. "You've got the wrong sequence here—the discovery of gunpowder was before the discovery of macaroni. It's pretty much agreed by history professors—"

"I know! I know!" Danny begins to hop around. "But it's also agreed by some *other* history professors that . . ."

Hector's listening. Then he just pops out with this rap song. "His-*to*-ry! To me it's my-*sto*-ry, why you don' start livin' in *this* cit-tee! 'Cause we is *now*, Ba-*by!*" And he spins around like Michael Jackson, ending up, "Whoo-ee!" in front of them.

Mark looks at him as though he's some kind of specimen and hides behind his *New York Times*.

Danny elbows his project to his desk, just missing the foot that John sticks out in front of him.

"I'm not comin' to school if that kid comes here! I'm sorry! My mother'd never let me an' I don' want those disgusting purple bumps on my face!" Denise is so nervous, she's cracking her gum like a type-writer.

Touching her foot-long rhinestone earring, Lisa looks up from under the pile of frizz. "Whaddya talkin' about?"

"I'm talkin' about this kid on TV. This kid that got AIDS."

"Fuh-get it. The neighborhood's never gonna let 'im come in heah."

Without definitely looking, I see Raymond coming in, his football jacket hanging off one finger. He's pushing that yellow swoop of hair out of his eyes and grinning because he's late. His grin is half em-barrassed, half sure that it's all right because he's Raymond.

I lean my chin on my hand. What if Raymond and me were *very* dear friends, and I had a terrible disease?

"It's so beautiful here in the park, Raymond, and I'm glad because I have something to tell you. But not now, not yet . . ."

"Oh, you little silly, tell me. You know you can tell me anything."

"I know, but first come look at these darling baby ducks." I run down to the lake and he chases me. The sun is all lights and dazzly on my rich auburn hair, and my floaty white dress has a black velvet ribbon

around my teeny, delicate waist. Raymond could easily catch me and crush me. After all, he is star quarterback of Junior High 212. But he is so sensitive and shy, he won't even touch me on my arm!

We're laughing breathlessly by the edge of the water— I can feel his breathings he's so close. Quickly, I dash away. He follows. "Wouldn't you like a refreshment? Let me buy you whatever you want. A soft ice cream sundae? A burger with cheese and bacon? Oh, pardon me! I didn't mean to hurt you in your religious affiliations! I'll never eat bacon again!"

"You know I didn't mind if you do. I'll just have a single scoop of maple walnut, with sprinkles."

We're sitting at one of those little green wire tables and chairs that fit only two. Suddenly, he notices I'm crying. "What is it? Won't you tell me?"

I can't hide it any longer. "Raymond . . . I have a terrible disease."

"It doesn't matter!" he cries.

"But it does! It's too late for us." Now we're both crying, it's so sad.

Mrs. Coopersmith taps her pencil on the desk. "I believe Laura has completed her assignment on the nature of courage. Is it personal, or may I read it to the class?"

I shrug. "If you want to. I don't care." I wonder if Raymond is listening?

"There are two kinds of courage. One is the kind we usually think about—two men, or two armies, meet and try to win over each other. It does take courage to know you've got to kill or be killed and not run away. Also, in sports, like football, it takes courage because you might be badly injured.

43

"But I believe there is another kind of courage. In *Julie of the Wolves*, when she finds out her Eskimo real father has killed her wolf father, she decides to keep on being Eskimo, even though there isn't any future chance for her people. Also, Anne Frank had to show a lot of courage just waiting in the hideaway."

My head is down, but I glance sideways. Is Raymond listening? It's hard to tell because *his* head is down. A silky yellow tussle of hair is all I see. Mrs. Coopersmith finishes my composition . . .

"So, for these reasons, I think that yes, it does take courage to fight, but in my opinion, sometimes it is harder and braver to fight like Anne Frank, and Julie and Karana, than the other way of fighting with guns, bombs, et cetera."

"So! You mean the Jews shouldn't fight back?" Danny starts waving his arms and his saliva is spraying out with his s's, he's so mad.

Before I can try to explain to Danny I didn't mean exactly that, Mrs. Coopersmith holds up her hand.

"What Laura is saying is a difficult idea to grasp. It brings to mind a poem of Emily Dickinson that could be very appropriate here:

> "To fight aloud is very brave,
> But gallanter, I know,
> Who charge within the bosom,
> The cavalry of woe."

Mrs. Coopersmith says it "boo-sum."

"What does that mean?" John asks, suspicious like he might have to punch somebody.

44

I, myself, am not sure about "cavalry of woe" charging in the boo-sum.

"Hey!" Hector says. "Light'n up! Too much boo-sums of woe aroun' here."

"Yeah," Lisa says. "You tol' us did we like mysteries, aventures, stories like that. Why can't we do somethin' else?"

Mrs. Coopersmith sighs. "Perhaps this *is* too serious to stay with for long. But I do hope that you'll think about it in quiet times at home or walking to school."

Mysteries! Everybody is wild to do mysteries. Personally, I think they're boring because it's always a girl, or two girls and their boyfriends, who have to solve a case—*The Case of the Egyptian Mummy* or *The Case of the Haunted Windmill.*

Mrs. Coopersmith says, "Would you like to do reports on your favorite mysteries? Or write your own?"

"Write our own!"

"All right, then. Let's see what you can do."

I don't want to write anything, but my pencil is pulling on the reins, ready to run:

" 'Vanessa Redmond, Female Investigator,' was the sign on the office door. Vanessa threw back her rich auburn hair, cut in the long style, and sighed. You could see that she had on a pearlish pink blouse that went beautifully with her hair. Suddenly a bald-looking gentleman, with a derby hat . . .' "

I'm writing and writing, I have so many ideas!

"Denise?"

Denise wants to read hers. "My girlfren' and me were walking in the woods. Suddenly, they say

45

Watch Out a crazy man! He haves no face eksep white. We go screamin' and runnin'. When I get home my mother said why you go in the woods if I tell you no."

"My goodness!" says Mrs. Coopersmith. "That was quite an adventure!"

Danny is holding out a bunch of papers toward Mrs. Coopersmith. "Go right ahead, Daniel."

" 'The Adventure of the Limp-Footed Men.' Harry Hillman, detective, was sitting by the fireside when a loud knock came from the door. His keen nose curved toward the door. 'Who is it?' There stood a man of about five foot seven and one-half inches, who said, 'Good evening, Mr. Hillman.' 'Yes, why don't you come in as you seem to be limping. Did you get your injury in fighting in Africa?' The man asked in a surly way, 'How did you know?' 'It was simply by observing. First I noticed that you had eyes that were yellow in the white part. African fever. Second, there was a worn spot by the side of your trousers in the shape of a sword.'

"The man mentioned, 'Someone is following me.' 'Yes, I know. I observed it by looking out through the window. Two men, who also are limping are hanging around in the street outside. We must depart down the fire escape.' "

Mark interrupts. "He's just copying Sherlock Holmes."

"I am not! If you want to know—I have an uncle whose real name *is* Harry Hillman and he works for the New York City Police Department!"

Mrs. Coopersmith smiles and nods at Danny. "Go ahead with your fascinating story."

"Soon they were outside in the alley and Harry Hillman said, 'It will throw them off the trail if I pretend to limp also.' By concentrating, Harry Hillman could make wrinkles all over his face so he looked about seventy. That, plus limping, took away the men's suspicion and they jumped in a cab to the train station.

"After an hour or so, they arrived. It was a dark, old, small type of castle that the limping man, whose name turned out to be George Barley, took them to. The butler gave them some food and drinks and Harry Hillman said, 'I analyze that you are worried about something.' Suddenly there was a blood-curling scream and the butler fell down the whole steep stairs. They asked him if he fell or was pushed and he cried, 'Pushed!' When he got up, he also was limping."

For some reason, this is so funny the whole class goes hysterical. They're practically falling down from laughing, but I try to hold it in because I do *not* think you should be laughed at when you write something. Raymond isn't laughing either. Goodness! Poor dear, I think he's sleeping. He's probably practicing too hard. I hope he doesn't sprain himself.

"Continue please, Danny."

"Well, I haven't figured out yet how I'm going to finish it."

"Has anybody any suggestions? We have a very interesting clue here, that of the appearance of a number of limping men. What might he do with that? How might it end?"

Hector is drumming about two inches off his desk, moving his head to his inside Walkman. Without stopping, he says, "Could be a club a' some kind. 'Bout all you can do with that many limpin' guys. They could be in a club. Call 'em the Limpo-Maniacs."

Back to Vanessa Redmond: ". . . carelessly yet elegantly, Vanessa put her long, silk stocking legs out of the car . . ."

BAWWP!

I jump as if I just got an electric shock. This is a definite trouble with school. Just when you are deeply embraced with an idea—*Bawwp!* I grab for my books and join the shuffle to the hall, with Mrs. Coopersmith bellowing, "Tomorrow, we'll do the casting for our Christmas play!"

Usually, since third grade, play programs say: "The Mother—Laura Fine." But I still love doing plays.

ſIX

"Scrooge has the most lines," Mrs. Coopersmith says. "Who thinks he could conscientiously prepare all his speeches?" I adore *A Christmas Carol*. That's probably why I suddenly do this crazy thing—I raise my hand! "Ha! Ha! She thinks she's a boy!" Et cetera. All the silly remarks and jokes that you expect from seventh-grade kids. Nobody else wants to study all those lines, so I get the part.

Mrs. Coopersmith says, "We'll keep your hair under a cap, Laura, and we can age your face with makeup. I'm glad you volunteered. I wouldn't have thought of a girl playing Scrooge, and you'd be excellent in the role. Now, the next part is Tiny Tim. Please don't volunteer unless you are really prepared to work hard and know all your lines."

Nobody's volunteering so she looks at Danny. "I am not suggesting you because you happen to be the least tall in our class. I feel you would give a very good interpretation of the part. Will you take it?" Danny blinks like a nervous rabbit with eyeglasses. Then he says, "All right."

49

You see, kids really want to be in a play, but they're embarrassed because you have to go in front of everybody and act emotionally. I don't care because I love the story. I think it is amazing that Charles Dickens could get these ideas about ghosts and spirits, and funny names like Mr. Fezziwig. He writes so many words to say something. But that's the way British people talk. You get used to it.

"Nuh-uh!" Krystal says when Mrs. Coopersmith asks what part she'd like. "You're not gettin' *me* up there jumpin' aroun', ackin' like a fool."

Hector grabs the chains—it's Mrs. Coopersmith's dog's leash—and shakes them. "I am da ghos' of Jacob Marley!"

"Good!" says Mrs. Coopersmith. "Hector, you've come to warn Scrooge that if he continues to be so cruel and stingy to Bob Cratchit, his clerk, *and* street musicians, *and* just about everybody, he will be punished in the next life."

"He's supposed to scream when he rattles his chains," Danny says.

"I don' scream. I leave screamin' strickly to duh womens." Then Hector makes up a rap song right out of his head:

"Scrooge, if you can't give a dime to a brother,
Singin' in the gutter,
You end up under the stone,
Wit' nobody to moan.

"No offensives to you, Ms. Scrooge."

"Raymond, will you be Scrooge's nephew, Fred?"

Raymond shrugs. "OK." He's my nephew—that means we're relations!

"Henry Chen, we have a good part for you, the Ghost of Christmas Present."

"The Ghost of the Christmas Present?"

"Well, no. This is the ghost of Christmas *now*, in the present, that is. You would do it very well. See, here's the picture."

"He *would* be good! He looks smiley, jus' like that ole guy."

"John, because you are fairly tall and thin, you'd make a fine Ghost of Christmas Yet To Come. We won't see much of your face, but Denise—I'm sure she'll want to be our makeup person—Denise can make you up to be skeletal and ghostly under this long black hood."

"Hey! A skelekon! Couldn' we be skelekons, Mrs. Coopersmith? I'd be jumpin' all around, rattling my bones—Ooh! Ooh!" Some kid starts dancing like a skeleton.

"Sit down, stupid! This ain't Halloween. This is Christmas," the rest of the kids shout.

Christmas! It suddenly makes me worry. Should a person of my preference of religion be in a Christmas play? And practically the most important part? Is this being not faithful to the Jewish faith? I don't really think so because it's in a book. I'm sure Jewish people would love it if they just read it. After all, Mrs. Coopersmith is Jewish and she wouldn't do anything against the Jewish people. I feel better after thinking of those facts.

Should I try to do my part in the English style? Like when Scrooge says to the ghost of Jacob Marley, "You may be a bit of an underdone potato," I could say, "Poe-tie-toe." Better not. Kids could think I was snobbing them.

Denise is going crazy with the greasepaint sticks. Lisa begs her, "Do my face like Blonde Velvet!" And somebody else says, "Fix me like a werewolf!" This makes Mrs. Coopersmith pump herself up as tall as she can go. "Just a minute! Just a minute! If you behave like this, we will never be able to prepare this play in time for Christmas. I expect maturity from seventh graders and if we cannot have it, we will simply not do the play."

"Naw! Naw! We wanna do it!" Everybody stops bubbling around and starts looking serious.

"Mark, will you be Bob Cratchit?" Mrs. Coopersmith says. She *doesn't* say, "You look exactly like the picture, with your long, stick-ey legs, and your spindly, nozzle nose."

"I think we're ready to begin rehearsing. The first speech is by Scrooge's nephew, Fred, to his uncle. Laura and Raymond, come up here. Read your first line, Raymond." Fred/Raymond's face is "ruddy and handsome," just like Dickens wrote. I am trembling in all my arms and limbs. "A merry Christmas, Uncle! God save you!" Only Raymond reads it without the exclamation points. Maybe he's nervous to be in such close physical relations with me too?

"A little more cheerful and lively next time, Raymond, please. Laura, are you ready?"

"Bah! Humbug!" It comes out louder than I thought it would, and oh no! I think a little spray of spit came out too, and went on Raymond! But he just goes on reading. Maybe he didn't feel it. I pray he didn't!

A funny thing is happening. By the time we get to, "Every idiot who goes about with Merry Christmas on his lips should be boiled with his own pudding and buried with a stake of holly through his heart," I'm walking around the "stage," shaking my finger at "the audience." Even my eyebrows are acting!

"Hey! Laura's good," some kids say. And Mrs. Coopersmith nods. "Very good, Laura. Very good expression. Now, let's have the ghost of Jacob Marley. I'll go over it with you, Hector. And try not to be *too* enthusiastic. Remember, you're dead."

I sit down with this hot, rosy feeling all over from people liking how I acted. But then I get deeply worried—am I taking praises away from Raymond? Maybe he's thinking I'm not a feminine person because I was talking loud, like a man? But I had to! You can't read those words with your head down, just hurrying to finish. He is so ruddy and handsome, and he can play football and be a hero. I'm sure he wouldn't mind if I have a little fame too. Of course not! If you like somebody even a teeny speck, you want them to be happy too.

Lisa is asking me, "Laura, listen to my paht, wouldja? I say, 'He's in the dinin' room, suh. I'll show ya, if ya want, I mean, if ya please."

"That's really good, Lisa." Do I talk in the Queens accent like that? Do I say "paht" for "part"? After all, I am from Queens too. But I think because our restaurant is in Manhattan, and I go there a lot, I'm not so naive as a regular Queens person.

Mrs. Coopersmith wants me and Raymond again! I think of hushing down the way I do the part. But, no! That would be against the way Dickens wrote it. Raymond wouldn't want that. He looks so perfect for the part, especially with this tall black-construction-paper hat Mrs. Coopersmith puts on his head. It doesn't matter if he reads a little dully.

"Excellent, Laura. You're improving, Raymond," says Mrs. Coopersmith. "Mark and Danny, father and son, it's your turn." They come up front, snubbing each other with their elbows. "If he were my kid, I'd choke myself to death," Mark mutters.

"If you were my father, I'd chop myself to bits with an ax, and then I'd jump in the deepest part of the ocean!" Danny is squeaking like an angry hamster.

"How would your bits get to the ocean, Danny?" somebody wants to know.

"Boys!" Mrs. Coopersmith holds up her hand. "You don't have many lines to say to each other, but you must look as if you are a very loving father and son. Try moving closer to him, Danny. And Mark, you put your hand on his head. Here, use this yardstick for a crutch, Danny."

"He's breathing on me! Ech!" Danny cries.

"Stop it, both of you! Bob, raise your glass and say your first line . . ."

"A merry Christmas to us all, my dears. God bless us!"

"Good. Now, Tiny Tim."

"God bless us, everyone."

"This is a very important line. Say it again, slower and with real feeling."

Danny wriggles as if little crabs were pinching him.

"What *is* the trouble, Danny?" Mrs. Coopersmith asks.

"I want everyone to know that the Jewish God was first!" Danny bursts out.

Mrs. Coopersmith is quiet for a minute. "I don't think you need to feel uncomfortable about this, Danny. I celebrate Chanukah, but I've put on this play as long as I've been teaching. My students, Christian *and* Jewish, enjoy it for its warmth and compassion. And I do believe that it's saying, 'God bless us, everyone' to Christians and Jews, Muslims, Buddhists, and, yes, even atheists. Danny, dear, would you feel better if we gave the part to someone else? You can be the propmaster or publicity person."

I was right! Mrs. Coopersmith thinks like me! She is a good person.

Danny says, "It's OK."

Naturally, some of our kids are darker and lighter than others. When Denise starts to try makeup on Derek, she is serious, like a smile is against the law. She tries a little of one stick on his cheeks, and steps back. Then she touches a little lavender and rich brown on them. Derek's eyes get bigger and sparklier from mascara. She takes out her comb and messes with his curls so they're wild all over his head. Kids start screaming, "Woo-ee! Prince!" (Prince is a certain kind of rock star that looks dangerous, but he probably isn't.) Denise shoves a blackboard eraser in front of his face for a microphone. " 'Cherry Moon,' Prince!"

Mrs. Coopersmith comes down like a giant attacking beaver. "We can't have this. It will take all our efforts to do the play in time and *this* does not help!" She slaps the eraser back by the board.

"Awright, Mrs. Coopersmith, I won't do it no more," Denise says. "C'mon, John." She pushes him into the chair and starts working on the Ghost of Christmas Yet To Come. Everybody wants to watch. "No," Denise says, and she puts his black robe way over his head like a telephone booth so only she can look in.

"Laura, here's the nightgown and nightcap from last year," Mrs. Coopersmith says, handing me my costume. At least it has no waistline, but the cap is like a skinny piece of underwear!

"Yuh can look now," Denise says, and she pulls back John's hood. John is always white, with brown shadows under his eyes, but Denise has made them black all around, and whitened his face more, and put gray skeleton marks on his forehead and cheeks. Lisa shrieks, "Oh my God! He looks like he got AIDS! Don't let him near me!" John can't see himself so he's surprised. Then he's proud of scaring Lisa. "Aarrh!" He snaps his teeth at her like he's going to bite.

"Denise." Mrs. Coopersmith hurries over. "I think you have to do his makeup a little brighter, with less shadow around the eyes." Denise takes off John's face with cold cream fast.

"The period is almost over. Once more, Laura and Raymond."

"Come in, Uncle! I am so happy to see you!" Raymond reads.

BAWWP!

"Cast, practice your lines for next week!"

I'll encourage him a lot. I'll do little happy looks and smiles whenever he's saying his part. He won't mind that I do it better. I *know* he won't.

ʃEVEN

"This is Maria de Los Angeles," Ramon told Mom and Dad when he brought her to work at our house.

"Should we call her by the whole name?" I whispered to Ramon.

"Nah! Maria is plenty. You can forget about the angels. This is New York."

She is too short and strong for an angel, anyway. Even her hair is strong, and black, and her nose looks Indian and fierce (which she *definitely* is not). She is kind of a small, busy package of a person wrapped in an apron dress, with big, colored flowers all over it. Around the house she goes, in rubber flip-flops, spanking rugs and throwing buckets of water at the bathroom floor.

I wish I could ask her about her children and their personalities. She showed me a photo of the five of them, all standing straight with hands at their sides and hoping faces. But she is new from Colombia, South America, and speaks mostly only Spanish. When I get out of school at 3:30, she is at the window smiling and waiting for me.

Today, there is Martha too. I introduce them, with Martha saying, "I'm very pleased to meet you," and Maria smiling a lot. Then we go in my room and play records and talk till Maria calls us for supper. It's really good: onions and chicken and green peppers, fried in a certain way that gives a good taste even to the onions. Afterward, we sit in the living room in front of the TV. Maria really *loves* to watch *"You* Can Win A Fortune!" "Let's go in your room," Martha whispers.

9:00—Mom and Dad poke their heads in to say good night. They can't wait to go to bed, they're so tired. "Get a good night's rest," Mom tells us.

"We will. Close the door, please." But it's too late.

"Get her! She's trying to escape!" Mrs. Katz flattens out and pours her fat, furry self over the edge of my bed to the floor. Stopping for a second to give us an insulted stare, she gallops down the hall. Mrs. Katz does not like to gallop. She likes to sit with her back to you, thinking cat-thoughts. She does not like having CPR done to her, even though we just pretend to press on her chest.

You should *never* actually do cardiopulmonary resuscitation on a human being *or* an animal, unless it is guaranteed, fully one hundred percent unconscious. Yes, you can rescue animals with mouth-to-mouth breathing and CPR. I am hoping someday to do mouth-to-mouth breathing on a horse.

Martha flops over on her pink flannel stomach and sighs. "Oh, Laura, I don't think I could ever really do it, CPR, I mean."

"Yes you could, Martha." I always try to give Martha confidence. "Hey, *Scarface Woman* is on at nine-thirty! Let's watch."

58

"Your folks won't like it if we stay up that late, Laura."

"We'll be relaxing on our backs and resting all the time. And we'll keep the sound real low." There is a little TV in my room, and Mom and Dad sleep so hard from working in the restaurant, they wouldn't even hear. They're not the strict, strict type of parents anyway.

"It's only nine o'clock. What'll we do till then?"

Martha's more timid, so it's me that has to say, "Want to call up boys?"

She squeals, "Laura! You're crazy! Which one?"

"Who do *you* want to?"

"I don't know! Who do *you* want to?"

Martha's eyes get all maple-syrupy behind her glasses. Thinking about Ricky does that. I gaze at Martha's rosy, healthful face and her clean hair that hangs childishly from her barrettes. She always smells warm and round, like a nice bakery bun.

"Why don't you call up Ricky?" Martha turns pink flannel all over. "I'll get the phone book and be right back," I tell her.

Padding down the hall in my bare feet, I stop to peek in my parents' bedroom door. My dad is lying on his back, hands folded on his tummy. He looks like a rabbi giving a sermon, a sermon of snores. "Huhhhh, buh, buh, buh—haahh!" Mom's elbow gets him.

In the living room, Mrs. Katz is relaxing on the phone books like a fat lady in furry pajamas. I pull Queens from under her, dumping her onto Brooklyn. She looks at me and says, "What did I do to deserve this?" I guess she must have heard Aunt Gertrude say that to Uncle Murray.

Dropping the telephone book *smack* next to Martha, I command her, "Look up Westerheim. You know how to spell it."

"What if *he* answers?"

"Hang up, of course." We both trot our fingers up and down the pages.

It is always hard for me to look up things in the phone book or the dictionary. I keep getting whispered to by words along the way, like *terrier* when I'm not looking for it at all.

Terrier means earth dog because it digs for small, furred animals in the *terra*, which is the earth.

"Westerheim—ah ha! Here it is, one eighteen Crescent Drive."

Martha acts like electricity is coming out of the page. "I can't, Laura."

"Do you want me to?" She nods, miserably happy. *Bee-baw-dee-dee-dee-dee-dah.* "It's ringing." Martha snatches the phone. Her face goes from happy sun to sad moon. I can hear the empty ring too. Nobody's home.

"Hey!" I tell her. "It's nine-thirty—time for *Scarface Woman.* Have some munchies." I toss her the bag, flip off the light, and turn the channel. Lying crosswise on the bed, feet straight out, heads against the wall, we can watch TV in utter comfort. It's an old gray and white picture. The screen goes all tweedy and the sound has to hurry to catch up. "This is an old one. It's going to be *good.* Ahhh . . ." Music is getting louder. "Muriel Madison, in *Scarface Woman!*"

Muriel Madison's face, big as the screen, comes on first. It is like powdery marble and her mouth is a wide, dark piece of velvet cut out in the shape of lips. She has on a man's hat with a feather on the side and a man's suit with packed shoulders like a football player. "Weren't the movie stars funny-looking in those days," Martha says, but I don't answer. I don't feel you should talk while a movie is going on. It brings you back to your regular self too much, when you just are wishing to be melted into the screen.

Muriel Madison is about to be married to this really nice boyfriend. But she starts going with a gangster because he's, well let's face it, he's more exciting than her boyfriend. This gangster's got a hat like hers, but it dips over his eyes like a gray hawk, or maybe a hooded falcon.

Anyway, she gets a frame-up on her and she has to go to prison. But first this gangster holds her face against an iron and burns a horrible scar across her cheek. You could actually hear it sizzle! Martha and me hold onto each other at this part. "Disgusting!"

Then she hides in a laundry cart—she works in the laundry part of the prison—and escapes in the truck. Now you see the gangster in the nightclub he owns. He's smiling like he's so popular and successful. "This drink is on the house, boys," he says. When he goes in his office, she's waiting in the shadow with a gun. Only she looks like a man in her laundry uniform with the collar up and her hair pushed under the cap. "Who are you? What do you want?" And slowly she takes the collar down so he can see the scar. "I've been dreaming of only one thing, to kill you for what you've done." "No! No! I'll give you my nightclub. Anything!"

But she can't do it! She throws down the gun and runs crying into the dark. And she's running and running, and her cap gets lost and she bumps into—her first boyfriend! She tries to cover the scar, but he takes her hands away from her face. "I know. You don't have to hide from me. I still love you and I always will." "You mean . . . ?" "Yes. I've always been waiting for you." "You don't mind . . . this?" She touches the puckery scar. Instead of answering, he bows his head to her lips and it looks like he's taking a long drink. Music starts pouring all around. The End.

"How could he not mind the ugly scar?" Martha asks.

"Well," I say, dabbing on some Swiss Milk Neutralizer-Moisturizer—one of the customers gave Mom a free sample. It is *definitely not* a cosmetic. "Well, some men, probably most men, only want you if you are perfect. But there *could* be some person who is different, who is sort of shy and even though he's handsome, he's not like the others . . ."

"It's eleven-thirty! Are you girls *still* awake?" Daddy's in the doorway, his hair standing up in worried clumps. Even his nose looks worried. Ever since I've known him he has looked like that. I think he must have been worried even when he was a little baby.

"No, we're not awake!" we shriek, jumping in bed and throwing the covers over our heads.

"Go right to sleep. You've got school tomorrow," he says, pretending he's mad. He turns off the lamp and closes the door behind him.

Immediately, Martha is a soft bump with breathing going in and out.

*I close my eyes, then I open them again and see . . .
my room, my horse collection, in the bluish dark light.
The little crystal horses paw with their tiny hooves. The
wooden ones throw their necks proudly. They are herd-
ing themselves, making soft horse-talk through their
noses, muzzling each other. "Let's get on the trail for
Star Country!" I leap on Black Star, who is shiny in
the moonlight like black water. The great, strong cush-
ion on his back is under me. My knees press him to go
up. I raise my arm, and with a few last whinnying
dances, my herd of horses moves out after me.*

*We are running easily on the air, so there's no sound
of hooves. Blackness of earth and starshines are all we
see. I turn Black Star's mane to the side and down.
Something is pulling me.*

*The earth is coming up at us like when an airplane
is going down. It is day down there, afternoon, and a
long field is waiting, a football field.*

*Screams are coming up to me. But nobody is play-
ing. The team is still as chessmen and the cheerleaders
are crying. A cheerleader is spread out on the ground!*

*Nobody knows what to do. Black Star is whooshing
down over them and I put on the brakes—his front feet
rear up and we land. My riding boots stride over to the
fainted girl. (I'm also wearing a soft, airy pink kind of
dress that comes to just over my knees.)*

*Everybody moves back. I lean over, my ear to her
mouth—she's not breathing!* And *no pulse! I begin
rescue breathing and chest compressions immediately.
Calmly, without being nervous, I work. "One and two,
and three, and four . . . puff, puff."*

*My muscles are like rippling steel (but not the bulging
kind). "Press, release, press, release."*

"Her eyelids are moving!" somebody cries.

The girl opens her mouth and smiles at me. "Thank you!" she says.

I get to my feet. "It was nothing."

Then I see under the helmet of one of the football players the secretly smiling face of Raymond. His glance admires me. "I didn't know you could do such terrific things." Gaily, I leap onto Black Star and mount upward again, beckoning with a lighthearted smile to Raymond.

Now, he on his horse and me on mine are riding on a golden chiffon scarf of stars in the black velvet night. Till dawn, we play and race in the star fields . . .

"Laura! Laura! I'm hungry."

A rosy moon swings in front of my eyes—Martha's face.

EIGHT

Martha is spooning in Raisin 'N Banana Bran Bits. "I wonder what Ricky eats for breakfast?" she says, stopping her spoon for a moment. "Probably eggs and bacon and an English muffin with jelly." She begins to eat again.

"Hey, if you want eggs, I can still make you some, but not the bacon. It has nitrites in it."

"Nitrites? What's that?"

"It's a kind of poison they use to make the bacon not spoil before you buy it."

"You mean Ricky is eating *poison?*"

"Martha, we don't even know *what* he eats for breakfast."

What does Raymond like for breakfast? Definitely *not* dry cereal. Maybe eggs and ham or bacon, which I could never have, if, if we *ever* happened to be eating breakfast together, which could *never* in all this world, *ever* be. But I still wouldn't eat the bacon or ham part because of Grampa Raphael. He never told Mom and Dad or me not to do anything, even if it's against the Jewish religion. He's not like that.

And he'd never know. But I'd still say, "Thank you, Raymond. I shall have to eschew—that means avoid—this portion of your breakfast meal. It might hurt my grandfather's feelings. He is quite religious, you know."

Anyway, Raymond probably doesn't even have to eat breakfast. He could get a pizza, or grab a doughnut and an apple from the table as he runs out. "See ya, Dad! See ya, Mom!"

And he's running down their big lawn with one hand holding off the whole offending team. The cool ones are waiting for him. "Ay, Ray! Whatta ya say?"

"Laura, how come you don't talk very much about boys? Sometimes you look as if you could die for Raymond. *Everybody* knows. And you're in the play together and everything. Does he ever happen to touch against your arm when you're doing the parts?"

"Martha, *please!* I'll tell you a secret—I once thought about Raymond and me, well, you know . . . But Martha, we'd just be doomed. My Grampa Raphael probably could never get along with his snobby, rich father. And my mother and father, even though they probably wouldn't say anything, they'd be too hurt because he's of a different persuasion of religion. I'd just have to give him up."

"But, Laura . . ."

"I'd rather not talk about it. Do you want to watch 'The Morning Show' before we leave for school? We've got time." I snap it on quickly.

There they are, the man and the lady who never stop smiling and chatting while they're sitting on a couch. "There's been a terrible earthquake in Bolivia." Smile, smile. "Three thousand people have lost their jobs." Chat, chat.

"Isn't her sweater pretty with all those blue sequins? And her hair, how does she get it to stay in those big, wavy swirls?"

"I'll tell you, Martha, there's a man with a comb and a brush hiding under the couch. It's his job to run out and comb her up every four minutes."

"Oh," Martha says. She is an incredibly naive person.

Next, there's a rock star in a huge jacket on the couch with them. His pink and orange hair comes up out of the jacket like a stiff fountain. "Really. It's like, uh, great," he says when they ask him how he feels about his famousness and success.

"I think Jon Bon Jovi is much cuter." Martha starts doing some homework.

Suddenly, a mom and her baby are smiling and the baby is hugging a roll of toilet paper. "This is the only one soft enough for *my* little Tracy."

Then there's a boy standing in front of a plain white wooden house somewhere with his mother's arm around his shoulder. He has a white face and brown eyes and very neat, combed brown hair. Except for being whiter and thinner, he looks like any regular kid. The couch man is saying, "The case of a twelve-year-old boy who acquired the fatal disease AIDS from a blood transfusion came before the State Supreme Court last week." Zoom—the camera goes right up close in the boy's eyes. I snap off the TV *fast*.

"Laura, wait! Don't turn it off. I want to see more about the AIDS boy."

67

"All right, Martha, but you'll be sorry. It doesn't do any good to keep hearing about it. It just makes you feel scared and terrible." But by now they're on a dog that makes beer commercials and gets thousands of dollars. "Come on, Martha, we'll be late."

Hurrying down the walk, Martha says, "Do you think he knows it's him?"

"Who?"

"The AIDS boy."

"Of course he knows! He's right there on TV. My goodness, Martha."

"I mean, maybe his mother could not let him look at the TV. And then maybe he wouldn't have to know it was him, that maybe, might, you know, die. Laura, could twelve-year-old girls get it? I haven't seen any twelve-year-old girls on TV that got AIDS, have you?"

"Germs don't care if you're a boy or a girl. Let's not talk about it anymore, would you *please*, Martha?"

"All right, I won't even think about it anymore."

"Oops! Sorry, Laura. Wrong girl. I thought you were somebody else." It's Eduardo. He's two kids behind me in the cafeteria line, and it was him secretly yanking on my hair. I smile and say, "That's OK," and turn back to deciding if I'll have fruit cup or vanilla ice cream. I'm allowed to buy dessert, but I have to bring my lunch.

It was so exciting in sixth grade to have cafeteria, and I minded being just about the only brown-bag carrier. But I'm used to it now, and most school food goes in the trash barrels anyway. It doesn't have smells like a real person made it, and tasted it until it was right, and then said, "Ahh!"

"Laura! I didn't see you for such a long time! How're ya new classes? Got anybody cute in 'em?" Jennifer wiggles into the line next to me with her tray—French fries, diet grape soda, and a roll and butter.

"I'm dieting," she tells me. Jennifer doesn't have to diet: She has a tall, beautiful shape and beautiful raving black hair—maybe it's supposed to be *raven*, but it could be *raving* because it goes down and over her shoulders and back like a wild horse's. She was in my homeroom last year.

"It's so boring," she says. "Most of the boys in my class are little babies and runts."

I finally choose a scoop of vanilla ice cream and follow Jennifer to our table, after paying, of course.

"Hi, Laura!"

"Hi!"

LaTanya, Tiffany Kim, and Rohina are taking stuff off their trays and putting it on the table where we all used to sit together last year.

"Laura, sit next to *me*. I saved you a place." LaTanya pats the chair and I dump my tray down.

We all start talking at once, which is OK because you can hardly hear each other anyway. The poor teacher in charge has to keep yelling, "Hold it down! Who threw that? Pick it up, *Eduardo!* All right, I'll get Mr. Bender in here."

I think kids can only sit still in class for a morning. Then they have to fool around and laugh and throw bunched-up paper. Boys do, anyway. Girls like to chatter a lot and watch everything.

69

"Laura, you still gettin' that ol' wheat bread? Then I can't trade you 'cause I'll get too healthy. Here, you want a bite of my baloney sandwich?"

LaTanya's sandwich is so good, even though it's got nitrites.

"Your hair looks cute," I tell Tiffany.

"Really? You like it?"

Tiffany looks surprised and pleased. Her parents are from Korea and they are not very modern. So she must have had to beg them to get her hair cut.

A candy bar wrapper lands on Jennifer's fries.

"Get lost, Eduardo!"

She looks utterly bored. I wouldn't be. I'd kind of like it if boys threw papers at me. Ah well, I might suddenly bloom like Anne in *Anne of Green Gables* and surprise everybody (including myself).

"Did you see Mr. Petruccio walking down the hall with Miss Block? He's practically kissing her with his eyes."

"Jennifer!" (In a made-for-TV movie, *Borrowed Love*, somebody said that.)

"I wish he'd walk me to my class. I think he's *so* cute!"

"Jennifer he *is* an *older man*. He's even too old for you."

Jennifer starts combing her hair to show she's ready to walk down the hall with Mr. Petruccio.

Compared to most teachers, Mr. Petruccio is actually pretty young. He tries to act seriously so kids will respect him. But it's hard to receive respect when girls moan and sigh after you as you're going down the hall. They also discuss his total clothing and ties every day. There's a little bare spot starting

70

on top of Mr. Petruccio's head, which Jennifer says she's going to pat someday! But the rest of him is hairy and smells attractingly of Old Spice man's soap. He even has hair on the back of his hands. Jennifer says that's *very* sexy.

"Hey! What are y'all gonna wear to the dance? It's in only two weeks!"

"I'm deciding if I should wear this silver jumpsuit I got from my sister-in-law," says Jennifer. "It's practically bran-new, but I don't know if I want to waste it on these *baby*-boys."

"My dress, you're not gonna believe it! It's all a-lectric blue satin with rhymestones aroun' this scoop neck. An' I mean, scoop!" LaTanya shows us how much.

"Blue satin would look really good with your hair," I tell LaTanya. Hers is soft-black-cloudy all around her.

Everybody's chattering about their clothes for the dance. I wasn't even going, but that wouldn't be fair to Martha. She desperately wants to go and she needs me for her confidence.

"Laura, have you got your dress yet?"

I'm *almost* mad at Mom and Dad that I'll have to wear my pink shirtwaist. But it's real silk and I've hardly worn it except for my cousin's wedding. "I don't know what I'm wearing yet."

"Rohina, is your father gonna let you go?"

Rohina looks down at her lunch. "Maybe. If they will keep boys on the other side and the teachers are looking."

"What good is that! What would you go to the dance for anyway? You too, Tiffany?" Tiffany nods sadly.

"Oh God! I couldn' stand it if my father was like that!"

I poke Jennifer under the table. "She can't help it."

"Oh yeah. Ya wanna go outside? There's still fifteen minutes."

"No. It's gettin' empty here and we have to talk about somethin'," LaTanya says.

"What?"

"Can't you guess?"

"No! Tell us!"

Tiffany looks worried and Jennifer moves closer.

"No! Tell us!" comes Eduardo's voice under the table.

Now we're all screaming and banging Eduardo with our books, and even a cafeteria tray. That is, I don't do the hitting part. Me and Tiffany and Rohina are too shy to do anything but the screaming. Jennifer and LaTanya are pulling his hair and squealing. "You rat! We'll kill you!" He's laughing while they push him out on the playground.

When they come back and sit down we all huddle around LaTanya. Inside, I'm saying, "Oh no! S-E-X! It's going to be about S-E-X and bodily parts. That is the most bothering word in the whole world. It's everywhere, and you're not supposed to know about it, but everyone does, even innocent, shy people like Rohina and Tiffany, and my mom and dad. There has to be sex, otherwise there wouldn't be babies. I wish I could live my whole life without thinking about it, but they won't let you."

LaTanya says, "Y'all been seein' on the TV about the AIDS?"

We all nod.

"I can't ask nobody at home. They all think I'm some little girl. But . . . can you get it from if a boy was jus' breathin' in your neck?"

"What boy?"

"Jus' a boy. If a boy sittin' next to you on the bus was breathin' on your neck, do you supposed to use one of those things?"

"What things?"

"I know," Jennifer says. "I see 'em in the park on the ground all the time."

I don't. What are they talking about?

"Laura, you are so naive! Look at her. She doesn't *know!*"

"Please," Rohina murmurs. "My parents wouldn't let me go out with my girlfriends, or do anything, if they knew I talk about these things."

"Well, honey, you have to know because we are all in bad danger, *especially* girls."

"I don't think it's girls. Only drug persons," Tiffany says.

"An' gay guys," says Jennifer.

"Well, I'm not gonna date *nobody* gay!" says La-Tanya.

"You couldn't. Gays just date each other." Jennifer thinks it's funny that LaTanya doesn't know. I don't know about gays, either. *Gay* means not to be sad. Why does that make other people so mad? Once, when our class was going to the museum, Lisa showed me two gay people. They looked so happy to be together. Just like I'd be with Raymond. What is so wrong about that?

"We're all goin' to have to be using them," Jennifer

73

says, opening her purse and beginning to file her nails.

What? What? I'm begging inside.

"Tell Laura, somebody, or she'll bust."

And Jennifer says, "You know those things on the ground, those skinny balloons? That's so you don't get bodily fluids."

LaTanya whispers in my ear like a dentist drilling. *"Bodily fluids*. That's what you don' wanna get."

"Oh," I say. I'm thinking desperately—if an AIDS person wants to cry, or do something on you, you mustn't let them. You must use one of those skinny balloons. How? Sort of like a raincoat, probably . . .

Praises to heavens! I could kiss Mr. Bender for ringing the bell!

NINE

"Here," Mark says, pushing a page out of his notebook at Mrs. Coopersmith. Never mind that he's interrupting her in practically the middle of "Piping Down the Valleys Wild" by William Blake, just where she's twinkling her eyes and playing her fingers up and down for the pipe.

At first, she's annoyed. Then she decides that she should look at Mark's paper in case he's contributing something to the class. "Hmm. This is very well written, indeed." Mark is jiggling his knee and looking worried while she's reading.

Now he gives the class one of his soupy smiles. "I just wanted you to see that I'm as good in poetry as I am in science."

"Well, Mark, this skillful rhyming is difficult to achieve. I have to admire how you've done it. Let me read it to the class:

"Eldorado

Gaily bedight . . ."

"That means dressed," Mark put in.

"A gallant knight.
In sunshine and in shadow,
Had journeyed long,
Singing a song,
In search of Eldorado.
But he grew old,
This knight so bold,
And on his heart a shadow
Fell as he found
No spot of ground
That looked like Eldorado.
And as his strength
Failed him at length,
He met a pilgrim shadow.
'Shadow,' said he,
'Where can it be—
This land of Eldorado?'
'Over the mountains of the Moon,
Down the valley of shadow,
Ride, boldly ride,'
The shade replied,
'If you seek for Eldorado.' "

Mrs. Coopersmith looks very puzzled. "There's nothing I could possibly say to improve this. Well done." And she hands it back to him, shaking her head. The kids, those who are listening, look at each other like, "Can you believe this?"

"How come this here 'gaily bedight' is hangin' out wid a pilgrim?" Hector asks. "The turkey mus' be lookin' for Thanksgivin'!" The kids scream. Not that it's so funny, but nobody really likes Mark. He thinks he's so great.

"Class! Class! Mr. Bender will be coming to find out what's going on. And you know what I've told you about respecting other people's work. It's library period. I know you'll proceed like young men and women through the halls."

I hold back a little, shuffling to the door. Raymond and Derek and Jamal sort of swing out of their seats, big and easy. *They* don't shuffle. They're *with* the rest of us, but Raymond is the prince in disguise. Oh, he's wearing jeans and a tee shirt like everybody else, but he has that grin. It's like the movie, *The Thief of Bagdad*. All the slaves are milling around the town in puffed white pants and turbans. Everyone's face and chest is painted brown, but only one is grinning like a prince. You'd know him among a million slaves.

Lisa and Denise sort of sway along. (They don't shuffle either.) They hug their books in front of them, their earrings are clanking. They're gabbling to each other, but their eyes are always circling, checking: What boy is looking at my new, oversize, fuzzy white sweater? Does he see how my Zou-Zou jeans fit tight-black around my legs?

Krystal is being herded to the library with the rest of us prisoners. But they can't ever capture Krystal. As soon as we're there, she sits on a chair and majestically goes to sleep. Tall as a stork, bending forward with his loopy walk, here comes Mark. Danny scurries in front of him. Now, he's a crazy beaver piling up stacks of library books and digging and scratching among them. He seems especially nervous.

It's a whole beautiful restaurant here, with deli-

77

cious books. Which should I have first? Should I munch on some poetry? Or take a big gulp of funny *Harriet, the Spy?* Or seriously stuff myself on *Jane Eyre,* and then for a dessert, a sweet bite of a fairy tale? I always wait a little, like when I was a little girl, saving the Hershey's bar Grampa Raphael gave me before I ate it. Then, I pick *Black Beauty* from the shelf. The people and the horses all sound as if they were writing letters to each other when they talk, but it doesn't matter. There isn't *anybody* who could be cruel to a horse if *only* they'd read *Black Beauty.*

I can touch the white star on Beauty's forehead, almost feel the soft, wet nose whiffling my palm.

"Ha!" shouts Danny, knocking his glasses off, he's so excited. The librarian gives him a crunching stare. Then he comes up to the desk and asks if he can use the copy machine for his homework. Slapping a big reference book on the copier, he's grinning like a maniac. Then he goes back to his seat, where for the rest of the period he's tearing up paper into small pieces and writing on them.

Just as the bell is ringing, Danny runs around and gives out the pieces to everybody in English 109. He's cackling madly while he's doing it. Mine says, "Meet me outside the gym at 3:00 if you want to hear about a secret crime that is going to be revealed."

"Hey, lil' man," says Hector. "What's dis secret crime? Somebody stole da 'raser off ya pencil?"

"He gots cockroaches in his head from too much studyin'."

"Maybe he got reincarnationed into Sherlock Holmes."

78

Danny's so in love with his secret crime, he's not even listening. He runs out into the hall and I see him dance like an Indian that's just caught a scalp before he speeds for his locker.

We're all standing around deciding whether we'll go or not. The girls mostly think Danny's a little kid with a big brain. "God, he's so"—Lisa chews the word like it's bubble gum—"imma-*chu*-ah."

I know *I'll* go. If a secret crime is going to be revealed, I want to be there. All through homeroom, kids are saying that Danny's the Mad Scientist and Super-Nerd. Hector says, "I gots t'ree chicks waitin' for me on t'ree diff'ent corners. I gots to *mo-ove.*"

But just about everybody shows up except Raymond. He's practicing out on the field. Being on the team makes secret crimes kind of childish, I guess. Danny is down in front of the bleachers jittering around. Girls lazy down the concrete steps. Boys jump four at once, chips flying out of the bags they're holding, which gives them the idea to sprinkle Fritos on girls' heads. "It's snowing!"

Lisa and Denise are sitting and reaching into their potato chip bags, tweezing them out one at a time with long, red-pointy fingers. They turn. "Cut it out!" They turn back. "*So* disgusting." But they both have the same smile. I'm embarrassed. I realize I'm eating my corn chips out of my hand like a horse, but nobody is exactly interested.

"Come on! Let's get this show going!"

"He probably doesn't even have any secret crime."

"All right, Danny, I'm leaving!"

Danny's walking up and down, pulling on his chin as if it was a beard. He raises his finger in the air.

"I'm waiting for the crime perpetrator, who is not here yet, to show his appearance."

More kidding around—playing like little goats. That must be why it's called kidding. Somebody's books get tossed in a trash basket. John grabs Lisa's pink satin bombadier jacket with a silver sequined teddy bear on the back and runs out on the field. "Stoopid *an'* boring," she says, not even looking at him.

I lean my elbows on the bench in back and follow the utterly blue sky over to where the football team is little specks and dots and tiny roars. Which dot with running little legs is him? Oh Raymond, I hope you "have a good day" for the rest of your life! If I knew a Jewish prayer to protect over you, I'd say it.

"Ah ha!" yelps Danny. "Everybody is here. We can begin." I haven't been noticing who's here and who's missing, or who just came. Mark is separate, way in back, looking at us like a fish on the ice in the A & P. He always keeps apart from other kids.

Danny starts. "You all were there when a certain poem was read by a certain teacher in the English department of this certain junior high school. This poem, which I have just mentioned, resulted-ed"— he's so excited, he's stuttering—"in the teacher saying it was skillful and perfect, with meter and rhyme, and everything." Danny's walking up and down, like we're the jury and he's the district attorney. "Now, due to certain research, which I have done in the library right here in this certain junior high school . . ."

"You are a certain jerk," John yells.

"Hurry up with this boring stuff," kids are saying.

Danny merely gives John a pitying smile. "I am going to reveal something that will get even with this certain person for all the times he tried to say *somebody else* was stealing from other authors, and not being original, and even having plagiarism!" Danny takes out a xeroxed paper. His hands are shaking. "This is from the actual encyclopedia and there can be nothing truer than the encyclopedia because all the greatest, smartest people in the world wrote it."

By now, nobody is saying wisecracks anymore. It's like we just heard about a hit-and-run car accident and we are running to stare down at the body on the road. Only he's not on the road—he's on the last bench of the bleachers! The front row of heads turn. Danny is almost screaming now. "Eldorado! During the sixteenth century, many explorers came to the New World in search of Eldorado, the legendary kingdom of fabulous wealth!" He howls, "Et cetera! Et cetera! Et cetera!" Until he comes to "Gaily bedight, a gallant knight," not everybody is sure of what's happening.

"Ayyy." Hector stands up. "He lifted da pome outa' da encycle-o-pedia. It's a rotten pome—I t'ought maybe he wrote it hisself."

"Are you gonna tell?"

"I certainly am!" Danny's stamping his feet like Rumpelstiltskin. "If people can just steal anything they want, there will not be any justice. Criminals will think they can just go free. And especially if that criminal is always accusing that somebody else, like me, or Henry Chen, is copying!"

"Tell!" shouts John. "He thinks he's so smart!"

Why doesn't Mark leave? I look back, pretending I'm looking for somebody else. He is blinking and blinking behind his eyeglasses. Both his knees are jiggling up and down.

"We've got to have a complete trial," says Danny. "*I'll* be the judge because I did all the research and solving of the case."

"Whaddya want? You don't need no trial." Hector takes out his comb and flicks it through his hairstyle. Then he checks out the back with his hand.

"Well, what are we gonna do? I gotta watch 'Divorce Court' at four o'clock. Personally, I couldn' care less," Lisa says.

"Maybe we should vote?" somebody says.

"No! Because if you vote, you might vote him innocent and he'd get away with no punishment!" Danny squeals.

"You shouldn' give no trial. Evabody just say how he think," Krystal says. Her face stays still as black ebony. The others are chewing their nails or twisting all around on the benches.

"All right! Let each one say what they think. But hurry up because we've got to do something right away!" Danny glares up at the back bench. I can't believe this—Mark is still sitting there! But he's shrunk and gray like rain is washing him down the steps.

John jumps up. "If he's in the army, he gets dishonorable discharge and they throw him out a' the army."

"So, whaddya want?" Hector wants to know.

"Yeah, whatta ya wanna do?"

"Tell the teacher, of course." John sits.

Danny says, "Henry, you're next."

Henry has only a little unhappy smile. He looks down, then he says, "It does not hurt *me* if Mark does this thing. But others may not agree."

"Do you vote Yes or No?" Danny demands.

Henry smiles. "I don't know." Danny goes on impatiently to the next person.

"Denise? That is, if girls *have* any ideas except about their nail polish."

"You little mutt," says Lisa.

And Denise says, "C'mere so I can push your face in."

"Laura, ovah there, she gotta lot a' ideas," Hector says. But I don't know what to say. He *is* a gawk and an absolutely nauseous person, but I don't know what they are planning to do to him.

They say it is just whether or not to tell the teacher, or maybe even the principal. But except for Henry and maybe some girls, I feel as if the kids want to stamp and squash Mark like a spider. It's scary. "I have to think about it some more," I tell Hector.

"What's to think about? You either believe it's right to be honest or you don't," some kids say.

"Denise, c'mon, what do you think?"

Denise shoots a look at Mark. "He's a creep an' I don' like him. I don' like how he's always spyin' on otha' people. 'You stole this, an' you didn' get your own original idea, I seen it in this otha' book.' So far as I myself is concerned, he's just a jerk."

"What'll happen if we tell or if we don't?"

"He'll get suspended or expelled, even."

"How can you talk about you're not gonna tell what he did? Then you're a criminal yourself!"

83

"Whyn't we ask him why he did it?"

"Yeah."

"Ooh, he's just going to lie again!"

Danny's popping like the spots of grease on Daddy's hot griddle. But two kids go up like police and take Mark's arms and walk him down. He doesn't fight at all. He's a Raggedy Andy, but all weak and sick looking.

"Why did you do it? Didn't you know somebody was going to find it in the book?" Mark puts his eyes down and shakes his head to both questions. This boy with so many important words has lost all his strength of using them.

"Whaddya say, Laura, da word nut?" Hector's smiling so I know he doesn't mean it hurtfully.

"Well, I don't think people should be so worried about marks and tests. I mean, I know it's hard *not* to be, but it doesn't really prove anything. A person could be excellent in history or math and maybe he or she wouldn't be such a good cook, for instance. But I do think it's awful to steal an author of his rightful fruits! Only he or she could think of those special words and it's like stealing his living." I don't know what I really think should happen to Mark. If he gets expelled, that's too much punishment. If he just goes along as if nothing happened, that wouldn't be good for him either.

I think he's going to throw up, but instead words start coming out of Mark. "My mother expects me to get in the High School for the Gifted and Talented in the Sciences. She's telling all her friends. If I don't get in, I don't know what I'm going to do!" Then, he starts crying.

84

"Oh God, what a baby!" John is disgusted.

"If his mother wants 'a get in the Gifted and Talented so much, let *her* take the tests and go!" somebody yells out.

"Ooh! Ooh! He's doing it just to get pity." Danny hits himself in the forehead and looks around desperately. "Vote! Vote! Everybody should vote!" he yells.

I begin tearing little strips of paper because I believe in the sacred secretness of the ballot. If it isn't, kids will just vote like their best friends or even be scared to vote the way they really feel. We had that in sixth-grade history with Mr. Donato. "If you think we should tell, put an *X*. If you don't, then put a circle."

Now everybody starts rubbing their foreheads and looking around, trying to peek if the others are doing an *X* or a *O* with their pencil. Mark is curled over with his knees under his chin, as if his stuffing has all leaked out. The strips are collected. Danny holds each one up and counts. "One *X*, one circle. Two *X*'s! Three *X*'s! Four *X*'s! Two circles." Hector didn't vote. When they handed him the strip of paper, he crumpled it. "Nah."

Danny is still counting with triumph. Hector gets to his feet, slowly puts his jacket collar up in the back, and reaches over Danny's shoulder. "Gimme dat, little bro." And he's got all the votes, plus the xerox from the encyclopedia.

"Hey! What are you doing?" Danny squeaks.

"Fuh-get it, fuh-get it. Dis guy wants 'a get in the Gifted and Talented so bad, let him. He still gonna be a sucker. He still gonna be pity-ful. What's 'a difference to you, he's a sucker here, or ovuh deah?" Hector takes a match out of his pocket, the kind from cigarettes, and he tears one. Zip, the flame jumps out. He lifts the papers high and holds the match to the corner. We watch the fast creeping fire that makes the words fall away in the air. Then he tosses the black flakes into the trash can and moves out across the field. His box is boom-crackling "La Bamba" when he goes through the field gate.

Kids trickle off one by one. Well, Denise and Lisa leave together, but they're not even talking. Nobody looks at Mark, except Krystal. She gazes at him, not mean or anything, but like a mountain gazes down at a river. Then she's gone. Going through the gate, Danny seems like an old little man with a big briefcase. I follow him, carefully not looking at Mark.

Do you want to know if I scratched an *X* or a circle? It was a circle.

TEN

Martha and me are here at the mall looking at dresses for the seventh-grade dance. We know our parents will say, "You already have good dresses." But still, there's no harm to look.

First we go to the record store. It's the most exciting place in the mall and all the kids have to check it out.

"There she is, Laura! Blonde Velvet!"

The most famous person in America, more than the president, more than Lincoln. Her name is really Mary-Ann, but she actually looks all blonde and velvety. I don't know why, but I feel embarrassed looking up at her huge picture. It's flapping over the whole record store, so she's two stories tall.

She is very beautiful but weird. How could you have a talk with somebody who is bending her head way back like that? I don't understand her, but Marth and me *say* we like her the best. I really like Julie of the Wolves and Karana better.

"Laura, look at that little black spot on her face. For anybody else it would be ugly, but it just makes her more pretty." I nod. Looking up, I think she is the beautiful goddess in the myths who eats up all the young men that come to suitor her, the ones who come to beg her to marry them, I mean.

Martha has to go through all the Bon Jovi records to check if there are any new ones. So I go stand in the doorway in case—just in case—somebody should be in the mall today.

Outside, Lisa and Denise are using the record store window for a mirror and they're combing away. "God, ya so lucky, Laura. Ya don' care whatcha look like," says Denise.

"She means ya not in-ter-ested, right, Laura?"

"Oh, yeah. That's what I mean," Denise says.

I do care! I'm *not* interested in makeup and things that hurt the animals. And I think people's hair looks silly all sprayed up in stiff pokes on their head. It's just that I believe there are other things a boy might want—like friendship and faithfulness, for instance. Inside his heart, I know Raymond does.

Martha's through looking. "Beat you to the escalator, Laura!" Whenever Martha and me come to the mall, we get giggle attacks. We ride up and down the escalators, imagining someone is riding the escalator too, looking for us, hoping to meet a Martha and a Laura. I guess Martha pretends it's Ricky. And me? Oh, just a blond, shy boy in a Number 10 football jacket that's maybe looking at sweatshirts in the window and eating a Dairy Delight. It's heavenly being in the play with Raymond, but he's shy to me as ever. Maybe it's all the other people being around.

Gazing down from the escalator, we see all the shops, and jungle-green plants, and shopping people sitting down on the benches in the middle to rest or feed their little babies a giant pretzel. It could be day or night, winter or summer, because all the lights of the boutiques and Adidas stores and Pizza Palace keep flashing, and the green plants stay green even if there's snow outside.

"Let's look at Teen-Dream, Laura." After we pass Pizza Palace and The Sweat Shop, Martha and me stand staring into the huge window of Teen-Dream.

"If we could just have some of those outfits we'd be gorgeous, wouldn't we?" Martha says. The really alive-looking models are sitting in their yellow, and blue, and purple, and pink jeans, with their legs way apart. Mom says, "Don't sit like that, Laura, it doesn't look nice." But Mom is so innocent. She doesn't know how things *really* are today.

"Laura! Look at that mint green boy jacket! A boy jacket makes you look *so* cute," Martha says wishfully. "See, Laura, it's so big with those giant shoulders, it makes you look smaller and cuter. Boys can't tell you're fat." Neither Martha or me has a boy jacket.

Maybe I could ask for one for my birthday, which is practically here. "You know, Martha, my thirteenth birthday is only two weeks away. I'll be teen-aged!"

"You're so lucky. I have to wait till February. Would you wear *that* to the seventh-grade dance? *I* wouldn't." Martha points to this teeny, tiny little slip with shredded gold hanging off it—only it's really a dress. A giant gold curly wig is on the model's head and she's laughing with her head way back while a boy model is looking down her throat.

Their legs and knees are so long and smooth and skinny. Martha's and my knees are like potato knishes.

"Do you want to try something on?" I ask Martha.

"Ooh, I don't know. Which one?"

"Come on, let's go inside and see."

We ruffle the racks back and forth for a while, holding up things and asking each other, "Isn't this cute?" and putting them back.

"Martha, isn't this adorable?" I hold up a rose velvet dance dress, with all ruffles and puffs on the short, short skirt and a tube top with little diamond straps.

"I dare you to try it on, Laura!"

"All right, I will."

The lady in the dressing room looks like she needs a Pepto-Bismol when she sees us, but she gives me a plastic circle anyway. "Are you sure that's your type of style?"

"It's for my sixteen-year-old sister. She's the same size and I might want to give it to her for her birthday."

"Laura! You're crazy!" Martha whispers when the little swinging shutter doors close behind us.

"Maybe I am. Who cares?" I pet the rose velvet, then I pull off my skirt and blouse. "Martha, help me get this on. Steer me, will you?" We're halfway in, that is, I am, with my arms over my head, and Martha is pulling, first from below, then from where my head is. Somehow it won't go any further, either way.

"Ooh, Laura, I'm scared! This dress costs a lot. Suppose we ruin it?"

90

"Come on, Martha, just pull."

"Laura, where's your face? I don't want to choke you."

"Hurry up, Martha. I've got to get out of this. I'm getting paralyzed!"

"I better get the lady."

"All right, Martha, but hurry!"

I'm standing, feeling like a corn on the cob before the green part is zippered off. Luckily, the lady knows just how to unpeel me. Hanging up the dress and checking it, she gives us a withered stare—she has blue eye shadow on kind of old, alligator-skin eyelids. "Chub-ettes should *not* try on this style of a dress.

"I'm tellin' you, these kids today." We hear her talking to the cashier as we shrink away. We're so glad to get out of there!

"Let's go from the top to the bottom on the escalator *one* more time, then I've *got* to go. Maria will start worrying."

We rise up, up to the glass roof, looking down on all the people scurrying like an ant farm in the five layers of the mall. I can't wait anymore to see if his golden-helmet head is going up or coming down. "I've got to go, Martha."

"Laura, how can we go without . . . ?"

". . . a Dairy Delight!"

We squeal off the escalator, past Athlete's Foot, and pant into a booth at the Dairy Delight.

"Do you think it really has one-third less calories, the skinny-Delite? I mean, you should get one-third less fatter from eating it and we don't," Martha says. We're spooning down our hot fudge skinny sundaes, and I'm about to explain to her that it doesn't actually *make* you thinner, when I get frozen from horror. Sherry and Alex and Zoe and Raymond are joking and laughing into this place.

I droop myself over my skinny sundae in the special skinny cup that everybody knows is for the non-thin. If I could, I'd leave, but Martha is eating worshipingly. "Hurry up, Martha."

"You didn't finish yours, Laura. What's the matter?"

They actually go into the next booth, and tripledip, whip cream banana boats and Cokes glide over us on the way to their table. If Martha would only stop sighing and licking both sides of her spoon. She's got ice cream on her nose like a puppy. *So* embarrassing! But they're not going to bother with us, I'm sure.

Oh no! Sherry is twisting around and hanging over into our booth. "Laura, would you like to help this adorable, terrific person to get to go to the dance Friday? He has to have all his homework done, including last week's assignments, or he can't go." They're screaming and banging on the sides of the booth, this is so funny. "Raymond, show your face to the young lady. Come on! Well, anyhow, Laura, it's Raymond. See, we're all helping but there's stuff like this social studies question, 'What does the First Amendment mean to me?' Nobody wants to do that one because it's an essay, you know. So, could you?"

Martha's eyes are two *O*'s. "Laura, that's cheating!"

"No, Martha, because I'd only be saying what it means to me."

"How 'bout it, Laura?" Three heads are hanging over into our booth. Not Raymond's. He's too dignified.

"Well, I *could* tell you what it means to *me*. That could give him some ideas. He'd have to write it in his own words, of course."

"Of course!"

"Well . . . the First Amendment means a lot to me because without free speech you wouldn't have anything."

"C'mon, Ray! Get yourself up here and listen!"

"Uh, hi."

My chest feels so crowded I can hardly talk. I *don't* look in his eyes. "Free speech means you can say what you want even if all the important people are against you. That includes that everybody has a right to think their own thoughts and beliefs. Also, you can give a speech or print anything in your newspaper without worrying that they would put you in jail. 'Thoughts are free. You can't put them in prison,' my Grampa Raphael says. Except, there is one thing that a judge said. You're not allowed to shout 'Fire' in a crowded theater and start a panic unless there *is* a fire."

"Hey, that's good! Get it, Raymond? Put down what she said, only change it, of course. All *right*, Laura! You did a good deed. Raymond's gonna be at the dance, thanks to you." All the heads disappear.

"Laura, do you think you should have done that?"

"Oh yes, Martha. It's perfectly all right. It's not cheating at all. It's . . . tutoring. He's going to do it in his own words, don't you see?"

"Oh," says Martha. "I guess so."

93

"C'mon, I've *got* to go." We slide out of the booth and Martha buys a bag of chips to eat on the way. I usually do, but not now, in case their booth is looking.

I haven't got a bit of doubt about what I did. It would be a cruel and unusual punishment for Raymond *not* to go to the dance, which even the Constitution says is wrong.

Outside the mall, the sky is fierce blue, like banners and trumpets. I wish it would keep that color, but it's gone into plain supper-time navy when we reach our corner.

"See ya, Martha."

"See ya."

Maria de Los Angeles smiles out the window, waiting for me. When she opens the door, the smell of goldy-browned onions and peppers comes out of her like perfume. I see Mrs. Katz bent over her dish by the sink, chewing in little, quick cat-bites.

I go to bed early, with Mrs. Katz in my arms. "You can't get away till I'm asleep," I tell her. Then I know she will jump down and sit watching in the dark, dreaming about little, scattering, squirrelly things all night long.

Well, maybe it wasn't exactly right. But I wanted Raymond to see I'm *not* like Mark, that I'm not the type of person that just cares about grades and studying! I'm a fun person too!

I wouldn't expect him to actually dance with me or anything. But there are possibilities. There are possibilities.

ELEVEN

"You look so nice, Martha! You look really adorable!"

"Do I, Laura? You don't think this skirt looks dumb? It's too long, I think."

"No. It looks perfect with the blouse. And that little locket with a lady's face on it is so pretty!"

"It's a cameo. My mother said I could wear it just for tonight. It was her mother's."

Martha's got on a white blouse with a little round collar and a ruffle on the front. It's so airy you can faintly see through it.

"Laura, you can see my slip straps. Is that all right?"

"Of course! That's the way you're supposed to be for a dance."

"Martha, come inside the door. Don't you look nice!"

Daddy's home early with Mom so he can drive Martha and me to THE DANCE. Just saying it gives me little shiny shivers. I'm not exactly dressed in a rose satin–velvet evening gown—it's my shirtwaist, but it's pink.

And, "Look Martha!"—I point down to my feet—"Black patent-leather pumps with three-quarter-inch heels." (I asked the shoe man why it had the name pumps, but he didn't know.)

"Oh, Laura, what does it feel like?"

"Well, at first they feel weird, like you can't really walk. You look down and it's a lady's feet instead of yours. Then you get used to it. I *love* them. But flats are definitely *in* this year, Martha. Most people probably will be wearing flats."

"Let's get these two princesses to the ball. All the boys will be waiting."

"Dad-*ee!*"

"Leonard, don't make them self-conscious. They're already nervous."

"What's to be nervous, two movie stars like this?"

We smooth our skirts carefully under us in the back of Daddy's car. Mostly we're quiet, looking out the window. Neither Martha or me are exactly good dancers. I mean, we practice privately in our rooms a lot, to Blonde Velvet and Bon Jovi records. But we're not like Jennifer or LaTanya. For them it's easy—dancing is just another method of talking to boys. For Martha and me it's hard to know what we're supposed to do, so we just try to keep wiggling a lot.

My mom says, "Don't be silly. All girls know how to dance. It comes naturally to you. When I was in school, I went to all the dances."

"How do you like your chauffeur, ladies?" Daddy says over his shoulder.

"Go slow, Daddy. We don't want to get there too fast."

"Ooh, yeah." Martha grabs my knee.

But when we get out of the car and see our ordinary yellow-brick block of a school all lit in the night, with kids hurrying up the steps, we hurry too.

"Thanks, Daddy."

"Thank you, Mr. Fine."

"I'll pick you up at ten-thirty, right here."

We crowd through the double doors calling to our friends, surprised at how utterly different and sort of wonderful we look. Everybody's hair is shiny and held with special barrettes, or scooped up on one side in a grown-up tail. The boys bump us out of the way, running ahead down the hall.

"You got manners like monkeys!" some girls shout.

But they do look handsome, even the funny-looking ones. And when we come through the swinging doors into the cafeteria, everyone sighs. "Ooh." A spell has been put on our cabbage-smelling, candy-wrappers-on-the-floor cafeteria.

It is mysteriously dark, but little firefly lights are tinkling down from the ceiling, and balloons are nodding and blooming everywhere. Kids stand around with friends, run to see other friends and scream, "You look gorgeous!" Then they stop for a second to worry if they look gorgeous too.

The boys are full of action, of course. They're punching other boys in the arm, grabbing sodas, and throwing popcorn up to catch in their mouths.

The long cafeteria tables have crepe-paper tablecloths and huge bowls of pretzels, chips, and cheese puffs. Giant soda bottles wait for the teachers who are the chaperones to set out the paper cups. Martha and I stand on the side watching. We're feeling little spiny tingles. This is a magic kingdom of night where everyone, even the just normally popular, is going to be happy. I don't see Raymond yet.

A teacher fixes the tape and the rock 'n' roll comes crashing on top of us. It jump starts your heart like Daddy's car when the battery's dead—"Ooh, ooh, ooh, I jus' wanna die! Open your heart to me, Baby! Open your heart to me!"

"It's Blonde Velvet," Martha and I say to each other. Boys are racing everywhere, picking girls to lead out onto the floor for dancing.

Martha and I head for a bright, chattery group that Jennifer is the silver jumpsuit star of, until two boys grab one of her silver arms and start pulling. She laughs and puts her finger on the dimple in her cheek, deciding which one will get her.

"Hi, Laura and Martha!"

LaTanya sees my shoes. "Congratulations! Laura's a big girl now!"

The girls are all laughing a lot and saying, "What a cute bracelet!" "I *like* your dress." But their eyes are sneaking around to where the boys are.

"Boys are so juvenile! They're scared to ask anybody to dance."

We all agree. "Yeah."

"So, who needs them?" Laila says, and she begins by herself. She is so attracting in her aqua pantsuit on top of pink needle heels that a boy starts throwing his arms around in front of her. That means they're dancing.

I see Hector with Conchita Perez, dancing close

together. Her black hair covers her face, then flies back so you can see her red geranium lips and beautiful black mascara eyes. Hardly anybody else from my English class is here. Lisa and Denise would think a seventh-grade dance is too babyish—"Ten o'clock it's ovuh? I'm just puttin' on my makeup to go out, ten o'clock. Chap-a-rones? You gotta be kiddin'!"

Ah! I see Raymond dancing with Zoe. He is so strong, twirling her in, tossing her out, grinning like Matt Dillon in *Tex*. Zoe is in a pink dress too, low in front, tight to her whole body, much more hot pink than mine. I could watch him forever, but, you know, I'm definitely, definitely glad Raymond would never ask me to dance. He'd be sure to find out I'm not any good. But at *least*, he'll chat a few words with me on account of the First Amendment.

"Laura, let's go get some pretzels."

"OK."

I'm not hungry, but Martha loves those little straight-stick pretzels. We sit on folding chairs by the food table. I'm amazed and astonished at seventh grade. They have transformed from "big for their age" girls and "small for their age" boys. There's this shy but sort of proud happiness coming out of them.

"I can't *believe* Shandra Singh!" I say to Martha.

"Really." Martha munches.

In the daytime, in school, Shandra looks so childish. She always wears an unfitting navy blue pleated skirt, a white blouse, and a gray coat sweater. Mostly she goes through the halls with her eyes down. Tonight she's in a long red, silky style of dress that models over her little bra and comes down to doll-sized white sandals. Stacks of silver bracelets are on both her little, delicate arms, and she's got a big red velvet flower in her hair. A lavender-velvet girlfriend pulls her by the hand and they go running like two butterflies in India.

Mainly, the girls stay in flocks like pigeons, twittering and gazing their little heads around. What they are looking for, of course, is boys, not food. Except for Martha, they hardly eat anything. The boys go running and sliding in their new shoes from one flock to another. So juvenile!

Andrew is putting popcorn down girls' dresses. "*Very* funny, Andrew. What a jerk!"

Most boys have jackets like their father's. They have father-sized ties too, or gold chains. Even if they are dressed grown-up, they still act like long-leg, loose-footed puppies.

Martha pokes me every time Ricky dances by, smiling at each girl, saying exactly the same remarks, it looks like. (Raymond is dancing with Sherry.)

"You know, it's probably better, Martha, if you don't know a boy too familiarly. You might not like Ricky as much if you did."

"Oh, I *would* like Ricky, Laura! I know I would!"

Somebody is tapping on my back. "Laura, would you care for a dance?"

I turn to see if it is . . . it is . . . Jonathan Berman. He's standing there with his stretched-out rubber-band arms and legs from growing so much, and his big, stare-y brown eyes, due to contact lenses.

"I guess so."

For a while, we stand in front of each other, jerking our arms and legs as hard as we can. When the music finally stops, he asks, "Would you like some refreshments?" He leads me to the cheese puffs and sodas. I choose Pepsi, Jonathan is 7-up, and we sit down holding our cups.

"Do you like your English class this term?"

He's a nice person, so I try to smile and be chatty.

"I think Mrs. Coopersmith's a good teacher even if she is sort of hyperactive."

He laughs as if I'm very hilarious—it's his nervousness, probably. There's no use my saying, like most girls would, that studying and books are boring. Jonathan knows from sixth grade that I'm Laura, the word nut. He *likes* girls like me!

"What book did you bring in for your favorite?" I ask him.

"*Boy of the Satellite* and *The Yearling*. They're my favorites."

"Didn't you get angry that his father and mother made him kill his deer? I couldn't stand it!"

"I know, but it's really better if one deer dies than a whole human family."

I guess he's right, but I could never have pulled the gun on my own fawn. I *have* to get away, or Raymond will think Jonathan Berman is my boyfriend!

"Oh look what Jennifer's doing! I've got to go see!"

And I rush over to where Jennifer's girlfriends are giving small screams with their hands on their mouths, and pointing at her. Jennifer is shaking her hair down her back and marching up to Mr. Petruccio. I'm safe in the giggle of girls where Jonathan wouldn't dream of following. I start screaming, "Oh no!" too.

Mr. Petruccio smiles under his serious eyebrows and they actually go where there's a space and start dancing! Luckily, he doesn't have to touch her—it's not a touch-dance song. Jennifer starts doing all these incredible show-off steps and Mr. Petruccio does them back. Kids clap and cheer, which makes Jennifer go wilder.

Finally Mr. Petruccio shakes his head and holds up his hands. "You win—I need a rest!"

And everybody is shouting, "All *right*, Mr. Petruccio!"

I find Martha again by the potato chips.

"Ooh, Laura, what'll I do if Herman asks me to dance with him? He's coming over here." Herman is in her French class.

"Dance with him, of course, silly. You have to get experience."

Raymond is dancing with Sherry.

I sip my Pepsi as if I'm enjoying it a lot. What if I just casually glide over to him and say, "Hi, Ray. How's your First Amendment?" Oh no! *That* would be awful! It sounds like something bodily!

Martha's back.

"His hands were all perspired. And he kept getting in my way so I couldn't dance right. I hope he doesn't ask me again!"

But Herman does and Martha gets led away, and back to her chair again.

For ages Martha and I sit watching. She's completely happy that she can just be where Ricky is.

"That's eight girls he's danced with, Laura." (Raymond is dancing with Zoe.)

"Potato chip crumbs are on your ruffle, Martha." I dust them away.

"Enjoying yourself, Laura?" Miss Block touches my arm.

"Oh yes!" I nod enthusiastically. But my heart is getting so desperate! How could it be that we are both at the same dance and he can just pretend I'm not here?

"Let's go across to the other side, Martha."

Maybe on the other side it's different. What is it that makes kids *so* crazy-happy when they're dancing? It's hard to get through the bunches of them without being stamped by new loafers, and lots of little, bare, strappy gold and silver sandals. Pumps don't seem to be in the rage.

"Laura!" somebody screams, and clutches me in front of her. "Don't let them get me, Laura! They're tryin' to steal my flower and mess my hair!"

It's LaTanya escaping from a gang of boys. I protect her from Louis, who keeps fiercely saying, "Ha *ha!*" and reaching around me.

LaTanya shoves me into him and runs away squealing.

"I'm sorry, Louis."

" 'At's OK, Laura," and he's after her. I guess it's very enjoyable to run with boys chasing you like that.

Martha pats the folding chair next to her. "I saved you a seat." There are at least twenty empty chairs! She is *so* naive! Sometimes she almost drives me crazy.

"Whadda ya say, Miss Word Nut, wanna dance?" Hector is standing in all light blue in front of me—a huge, floppy, blue bow tie and a blue, ruffly-front shirt, with a matching shiny blue sash wrapped tight around him in the middle, and blue pants and jacket. I don't say anything, I'm so astonished at his magnificent appearance.

"Notice da color-co-ordinated a-cessories." He fixes a blue flower in his lapel.

"Oh Hector, you look beautiful, even your shoes!" They're pale blue loafers. "But I don't really know how to do this type of dancing."

"C'mon, you can do it." Hector pulls me to my feet and out of the dark part into one of the puddles of light on the floor. I don't mean he yanks me or is rough, but it's as if he *knows* I can do this.

"Oh Hector, you'll see how terrible I am . . ." gets buried under "Rock Around the Clock."

Hector starts laughing his eyes at me. "Go, Laura, go!"

I think Vanessa has jumped into my three-quarter-inch heels! Hector is twirling me and throwing me in and out, like Raymond did with Zoe.

Look everybody! Look, Raymond! Laura Leonora Fine the word nut is dancing! It's so heavenly and wonderful, I try putting in some extra jumps and kicks. Kids' faces crowd on the dark edge, white smudges with big eyes. The little lights are tiny, rushing comets and the balloons are rising higher into the ceiling. Everybody must be watching! I wish it would never stop, but it does. The music gives an extra crash and it's over.

"I tol' you you can do it. Thank you, Miss Madame Laura." And Hector bows me an elegant bow with his hand in the front. Then he goes sliding off to throw his arm around Conchita Perez and wander her around.

"Laura!" Martha arrives breathlessly. "I didn't know you could dance like that! Everyone was watching!" (Was Raymond one of the white smudges?)

"Let's get a drink, Martha. I'm so thirsty!"

We sit by the refreshments and Martha says, "I couldn't eat another pretzel. But the cheese puffs are good. Have some. You must be worn out from all that dancing."

The chaperones are looking collapsed. Kids who are dates are hanging deeply onto each other, dancing the last dance slooow. It's 10:30 and Martha and me join the kids moving inchingly through the cafeteria doors. Jennifer and Louis call, "G'night, Laura!" I wave, too tired and happy to talk. Martha is happy too. She's so naive and innocent, I know kids wonder why she's my best friend.

Behind and all around, people are pushing and chattering. We are squeezing out the front doors and somebody, I don't recognize her voice, is laughing. "Oh my God! Did you see Laura dancing with Hector? I thought she was having a spastic attack!" Martha takes my hand and pulls us off into the dark by the side of the steps.

"I thought you were my friend, Martha! You should have told me I was dancing like a clown!" Big, fat tears are running off my nose. "And this stupid dress! I look like a ten-year-old!"

"You do not, Laura! You look pink, and elegant, and nice! And you were dancing really good. Hector wouldn't have kept dancing with you if you weren't.

Anyway, with that kind of dancing you have to act crazy like that. I wish you'd teach me how to do those steps."

"I don't know if I could, Martha. Suddenly, I just felt all these steps, and things. Maybe I won't ever again."

"Of course you will. Your dad's car is here, Laura. You want my handkerchief?"

It's dark in the back. Martha's telling Daddy, "Oh, we did have a nice time, Mr. Fine. Didn't we, Laura?"

"Are your shoes hurting, honey? I was a little worried because when you're dancing a lot, sometimes your shoes hurt, especially new ones."

"Not a bit, Daddy."

Martha squeezes my hand and whispers, "That girl might be one of Hector's girlfriends. And she was jealous."

"Uh, uh, Martha." I shake my head. But I feel better. If anyone wants to know why Martha is my best friend, this is why.

TWELVE

I'm *sure* what Martha says is true. Hector said, "I tol' you you can do it. Thank you, Miss Madame Laura." And Hector wouldn't lie. It was just an old girlfriend who was probably jealous.

I flip on the TV. So much news every single day, and it's never good news like, "All the countries have decided not to kill the whales anymore because they realize it is stupid, and hurting, and wrong."

Some lady with perfectly smiling teeth is telling us, "The twelve-year-old boy with AIDS . . ." Big snap-off! I don't know why they do this. It's just ruining everybody's life worrying about AIDS, AIDS, AIDS!

Mrs. Katz is there to gaze into the refrigerator when I open the door for my lunch. I grab her up in my arms and kiss her little pink triangle nose, while she's pushing me away with her front paws. "Don't ever die, Mrs. Katz." Thank goodness, cats don't get AIDS! I dump her down on the linoleum and run for the door. "I'll be home soon!"

Outside, I run back again, shaking the knob to be

sure I locked the door. Martha is waiting for me at the corner.

"Do dreams mean anything, Laura?"

"Some people say they do."

"They do tell what's going to happen. I once heard of this case. It was about a family that was going to go on their vacation and their five-year-old child dreamed that a hotel was burning and it was the exact name of the one they were going to. And he couldn't even read or anything."

"So, did they go to that hotel on their vacation?"

"Yes, and the hotel burned down just like the dream said."

"Then what was the good of their child's having the dream if they didn't listen?"

"Well, it still shows that dreams can tell your future. Laura, I wonder if you could try to make yourself dream something and then it would have to come true?"

She's thinking about Ricky. Her eyes are going syrupy. "I tell you what, Martha. At supper time, you should start thinking only, Ricky, Ricky, Ricky!'"

"Laur-a!"

"When you're doing your homework, say to yourself, 'Ricky, Ricky.' When you're in bed, 'Ricky, Ricky.' Behind your eyes you should see a snapshot of Ricky. Go to sleep. The picture is coming toward you. He'll say, 'I've always noticed you because you're quieter than the rest. You're the kind that doesn't only think about makeup and going out with boys. You don't need makeup because your cheeks are already pink. And your hair is nice and plain and shiny instead of sexy. I mean, it *is* sexy, but not too sexy!' Then he'll say, 'How about going on a date with me to Hamburger Heaven?' "

Martha's all blinky from happiness. You'd think a bride was walking on Major Francis Henry Sullivan Boulevard. Since she tries not to wear her glasses, she trips on a place where the sidewalk is cracked. We're picking up her books and she says, "Oh Laura, I know to most people it'd just be a joke, Ricky and me. But I am getting less of a pudge, aren't I?"

"Yep, Martha, you definitely are. And boys don't get married till they're at least out of high school, so you've got plenty of time."

The boulevard is going in a wide black river, past all the flat buildings till it bumps into the end of Queens. And right there, balanced on nothing, just like the Emerald City of Oz, is New York City. Every morning on my way to school, I still can't believe it. I look up and see the giant buildings holding their heads high and proud so they won't have to look down at plain, old, dumpy Queens.

Queens isn't a bad place to live, though. I really like all the brick two-family houses lined up like an army with arms straight at their sides. It's a good kind of army. It's my neighborhood, and Martha and I have walked to school every morning forever, since we were in kindergarten. It's safe. I mean, things are the way they're supposed to be. Families come out in the morning and go to work or school and come back again at night. It reminds me of the little round, wooden peg-people in kindergarten that fit in the right holes in their house and bus.

"Ayyy! Looka' these two chicks! What's happenin',

Laura? You findin' any new words?" Hector's already bouncing down the boulevard, flapping his hands and nodding his head to his Walkman. He wouldn't hear me anyway on account of the earphones, so I just smile.

He's not embarrassed of me a bit. See, Martha was right!

Here's good old yellow-brick Junior High 212. "Hurry up, Martha, or we'll be late."

Mrs. Coopersmith is not her usual self this morning. That is, she is not busying all around like the Little Red Hen. She sits watching each one of us come into the room. Lisa has black stockings with diamond spiders crawling all up and down, and Mrs. Coopersmith smiles softly when she sees them. Hector comes in. "My frens, do not be too loud with your English and stuff. I needs to relax myself from a' extremely cool party I was at las' night. My uncle got married!" Mrs. Coopersmith smiles at that too.

When we're all there, she stands in front. "I want to talk seriously with you about a topic that seems to be all around us these days, in the newspapers, on the television, in people's conversation when they get together. Can anybody guess what it is?"

"The Mets?" John says.

Mrs. Coopersmith smiles. "I wish it were."

Mark holds up his hand. "The AIDS epidemic?"

"I was gonna say that," Danny tells him.

She nods. "Now—it is highly unlikely that we will ever be confronted with this, but somewhere in this city a junior high school student with AIDS will be going to school. I think it would be good for us to talk about the issue—."

I suddenly say, "In the olden days, when they had these plagues all the time, the whole city died. Toby and Linnet and Alexander—they're in the Green Knowe books—were actually not alive, they were dead from the plague when Tolly, the boy, meets them.

"Tuberculosis was a plague too. TB, they called it. My Grampa Raphael once had a sister who had TB on the Lower East Side where they lived. And they used to help her when she was coughing and they loved her till she died. I bet I know what my Grampa Raphael would say if he were here: 'You know, the things you worry about the most never happen. Something *else* happens and you didn't even worry about it.'"

Raymond stands up in the back. His face looks so serious and strong. "None of you, except Jamal and Derek and me, knows how important it is to be in condition. We've been working out and training since we were in Little League. And we're not throwing it all away for some kid, who, let's face it, is probably going to die anyway."

Derek and Jamal start arguing with him. "Hey! Don't say *we're* saying that!" "That's cold, man!" And Mrs. Coopersmith says, "Surely, you don't mean that, Raymond."

I know how sports is to Raymond, but he *couldn't* have meant it the way it sounded! I hardly listen to what else they're saying about AIDS. I need time to go someplace and figure this out. I shrivel in the seat until the bell, and then run to my locker.

Spinning the combination, I feel a tall shadow over my shoulder. It's Raymond. He wants to explain—oh, wonderful! Then he's whispering hard in my ear. "You and your Grampa Raphael. Who cares what your crazy old grampa says? You're not a word nut, you're a word nerd! And you talk too much for a girl!"

My fingers are shaking and rattling the lock. When I finally get it open, I think I will creep inside the locker and hide. But I'm so nothing, I probably don't need to hide. I'm probably invisible. I can feel the air blowing right through and shivering me.

Oh Raymond, did you really say that?

Home! I run so fast, Martha can't catch me, and grabbing Mrs. Katz, I close the door to my room so Maria won't hear. Then I'm hugging Mrs. Katz and weeping into her fur. Weeping and sobbing both, because sobbing is louder. She flickers her ears on account of the wet, but she doesn't try to get away. Mrs. Katz knows how sad I am. A cat is kinder than Raymond. A piece of grass is kinder than Raymond!

"You know what he said, Mrs. Katz? He said I'm a nerd. That's the worst thing that can ever happen to anyone, to be a nerd. Nobody will want you except your parents. *And* Grampa Raphael, of course. 'So? A nothing called you a something! You are still my *shayneh maydeleh*,' I can hear him saying."

I cry and cry till I'm getting bored of crying for Raymond. My horses are watching, waiting for me to be finished. The windows are looking inside at me now; outside it's night. And a fried green pepper smell comes sneaking into my room, sent by Maria.

Jumping up, I shake my finger at Mrs. Katz. "I'll tell you what Raymond is. He's rotten to the pore!

112

He's mean! He's so mean, he'd kill a whale, or even a dolphin! Or eagles, or penguins, or any species. And it isn't playing football that makes him mean. Derek and Jamal play football and they're nice."

Then I walk around muttering, "Raymond, something is terribly the matter with you. Maybe you have problems: Your parents are so rich they don't love you, or they're too busy in their careers to talk to you, and that's what's making you so rotten, like in the TV After School Specials. I'm sorry for you, but I dislike you intensely. In fact, you revulse me. And Grampa Raphael is *not* crazy. He's a thousand times better than you because he's *good!*"

I march Mrs. Katz in to supper. We eat, with me giving some big, hiccup-y sighs into my plate, which I can't help. When we're watching TV on the sofa, Maria pats my head a little, and I move closer and lean against her till Mom and Dad come home.

THIRTEEN

Raymond is in my dream, and I'm crying. "Oh Raymond, I meant you so well! Couldn't we just be friends again?" My eyes jump open and my heart groans. *"Do* I talk too much for a girl?" Then I'm really awake. "No Raymond! Girls can talk as much as they want!" I'm free from being a slave for Raymond, watching if he's there, worrying if he thinks I'm fat!

I feel ten and a half pounds lighter in my personal self, that is, since I decided to eschew Raymond. At the corner, I grab Martha in a kooky dance and spin her around.

"Laur-a!"

But there is something strange this morning.

More mothers than usual are slamming their front doors and hurrying down the walks, holding onto their kids. Police cars are slipping by. I've never seen so many in this neighborhood. "Martha, do you think there's been a murder, or something?"

The lady from next door to Martha's backs out of her house, having a fight with a big piece of cardboard on a stick. "She looks like the chubby one in Laurel and Hardy, only she forgot her mustache!" Martha doesn't care for Mrs. Doppelman, so she laughs too.

Bigger kids are running from all the streets toward Junior High 212. Nobody is *that* excited about going to school. "What *is* going on, Laura? Maybe the school is burning down!"

"No, you'd hear the fire engines."

Mothers in street coats over peach-pink nighties and flowery housecoats are gathering in clumps. They'd never come out in their nighties unless something was *really* wrong. I don't recognize their faces, even though I *know* who they are. I mean, these are regular supermarket mothers—the kind that worry over which package of frozen chicken is cheaper; the one the little kid starts looking for when she's turned the corner with her cart and gone down the next aisle—"Ma-a-a-a!"

How can they look like this, like witches? If you hit a beehive with a stick, you'd get this sound, a hard growling in the air. Then I see Mrs. Doppelman's sign: "AIDS BOY GO HOME. WE DON'T WANT YOU IN OUR SCHOOL!" The mothers are like Medusas in their snaky pink curlers. I feel as if I'm being kicked in the stomach and Martha starts choking my arm.

"Laura!"

The air is breathless. The sidewalk trees want to run but they are stuck in concrete. Dying and death are coming to Junior High 212!

"What should we do, Laura?"

"Let's go to school, see if it's even true, and find

115

out what the other kids are going to do. Don't get scared, Martha. It may be just gossip that's not even true."

Martha's holding tight to my jacket and walking behind me. We really want to run away, but we are being terribly pulled, like magnets, toward school. Nearer, we can see a black herd of people on the lawn, mostly women, and police officers keeping them from going any farther. Mr. Bender is eating his mustache. He's clutching kids and hustling them up the steps and through the big doors.

"C'mon, man! We gonna be on TV!" Two boys push ahead of us like something's being given away free. The Channel 5 truck is parked on the grass and a camera is on top. An earphoned man is waiting. For what? The M16 rifles?

"Hurry up, girls!" Mr. Bender's grabby hands are on Martha and me and we're stumbling up the stairs with the last late kids.

"No AIDS here! No AIDS here!" the mothers are shouting. I look back for a second. Are they cheerleaders that suddenly got old and twisted in their faces?

The long, shiny halls and the banging lockers with rows of slits are the same. But how can it be the same if he's here? "Students! There will be no homeroom this morning. Go straight to your first class!" Martha scurries away. I run to English as if somebody were chasing me. Him? Mrs. Coopersmith is talking to the kids. She is calm, but her blouse is buttoned wrong.

"I'm late!"

"We know that, Laura. Sit down. We're discussing what is happening here today."

116

"Mrs. Coopersmith, why does he hafta come to *our* school?" Denise is practically crying.

"Denise, don't cry. We can think this through. It's not so terrible as you're imagining. When we don't know about something, we become fearful, and fear can create monsters out of mere rumor."

"This isn't no rumor, Mrs. Coopersmith! I seen the TV guys and the cops out front."

" 'I saw,' not 'I seen.' "

"OK, but he's still comin'."

Whamm! Mr. Bender crashes the door open. We all jump. "Mrs. Coopersmith! You've got to take over for Miss Giannelli in sixth grade. She's fainted and her class is going wild." This he says in a whisper you could hear in the next classroom. "Oh God!" He twirls his eyes around. "If I live through this day, it'll be a miracle."

"Boys and girls! Young men and young women! I know I can depend on you to be calm and grown-up. Keep on with the discussion and I'll be back as quickly as I can. Laura and Henry, take charge!"

"Why didn't they tell us? My mother would'a never let me come to school if she knew." Denise is sniffling and Lisa is sulking. I look at Henry. He is not smiling. Together we go up to the front. The trouble is, how can Henry and me take charge if we're scared too? I am, anyway, terribly terrified.

Suddenly, *crackle, crackle,* the intercom sprays Mr. Bender's fussy voice over our heads. "Students, we will omit the pledge to the flag and the singing of 'The Star-Spangled Banner' this morning. As you all know, in accordance with the State Supreme Court decision, a young person will be coming to our

117

school with AIDS. That is, he has contracted the disease AIDS, but he is *absolutely* no danger to anyone else. Health officials have assured us that under *no* circumstances in . . . err-uh . . . ordinary contact can this disease be transmitted to anyone else. I repeat: Under *no* circumstances can this disease be transmitted to anyone. You are being supplied with a helpful pamphlet from the Board of Education, which will be passed out for you to read and take home to your parents. It will answer all your questions. Stay calm—and have a good day." *Crackle, crackle.*

"Remember what Mrs. Coopersmith has said. We can think this through and you will see it is not so terrible as you are imagining." Henry bows his head toward me and actually smiles. He's smiling because he probably doesn't understand! I want to run out of this room, across the bridge, and all the way to the S & L! But Mrs. Coopersmith is depending on us.

"My mothuh isn't gonna let me come to school 'long as that AIDS kid is here." Lisa's picking off her perfect nail polish.

"Whaddya gonna do? Stay out of school the rest of your life?"

"Laura, you didn't say anything. What should we do?"

I don't know! All I know is, why does he have to come *here*, making kids afraid of their own school and neighborhood? If kids don't want him in their school, why does he have to go where he's not wanted?

"Laura, shouldn't he have a right to say where *he*

would like to be?" I see Grampa Raphael's kind little raisin eyes looking at me over his glass of tea.

"Henry and me are chairpersons. So, we shouldn't talk till everybody has a chance. Hector, what do you think we should do?"

"To me, this kid don' be Michael in *Friday the 13th*. Chill out. See wha's happenin'. That's what I do." Maybe Hector doesn't know about germs and viruses. Maybe his earphones and music protect him all around like magic armor. If only somebody would do something normal, raising their hands to go to the bathroom, maybe. But nobody does.

"Has anybody seen him? Does he have those purple things all over?"

"Nah, I saw him on TV. He just looks like a kid, that's all."

"How come they can just make our school have to take him?"

"There is a Constitution, you know!" Danny starts whirling his arms around. Behind his glasses his eyes are large as the bug's in *Science for the Junior High*. "This isn't Russia, where they can just do anything they want to you. My uncle, David Samuels, is a lawyer. He could take this to the Supreme Court."

"They already did that," Mark tells him. "And they found out it's discrimination if you don't let somebody go to school."

I don't want to do discrimination. It's just, well, disease is so awful. It takes your own body and makes it disgusting, or even dead! I know I could be brave if a little baby, or somebody's pet, was going out into the road and a giant oil truck was coming.

119

I'd hurl myself and knock the baby, or dog, or cat right out of the way. Myself, I might get some broken arms or something. I'd still do it.

The growling outside the windows is changing into a screaming. We run to look. "He's coming! Oh my God!" Back and forth the blue police push the screaming mothers. Like blind animals in a sack, they keep pushing out. Denise starts screaming.

"Oh, don't Denise!" I beg her. "You're scaring us more."

Two little dolls, a mother doll and a boy doll, are getting out of a big black car. The police make a tunnel for them to walk through. They are right under us and gone, inside the building.

"Please, please. If we behave this way, what will happen? Only more frightening things for everyone." Henry is trying to make us listen, but nobody does.

"Karana! I'm afraid!"

Lisa, so-tough Lisa, is sitting in her foot-long rhinestone earrings. They are like long tears. Down from her squeezed-shut eyes, two real tears are dropping. I have to make up a story, a Gramma story, so she'll stop crying.

"Lisa, there's all kinds of germs crawling all over you all the time. It's in the science book, in the chapter on 'Skin,' if you don't believe me. Your skin, right now, probably looks like the beach at Coney Island with a million, billion germs stretched on the sand, getting a suntan. Or maybe they're playing ball and jumping in the water and buying frozen custard. So a few more germs aren't going to hurt you." Lisa has stopped crying and she's watching me like a little kid. "I figure we shouldn't get *so* upset over this boy that we don't even know the name of. We should 'chill out,' like Hector says."

Do I really believe what I'm saying? I don't know!

Denise throws a wadded-up paper on the floor, hard. "Nobody—*nobody*—can make me go near that kid." *She's* crying now.

Everybody starts shouting again till Krystal starts talking, and they're so surprised they all shut up.

"Huh! Y'all talkin' a lot a' wimsy-wamsy words 'bout *that* boy. S'posin' it be you?" And she turns her back on the whole class and stares at the ceiling.

The slow roaring is coming here. We rush to the door. At the end of the hall, there are flashes and too many voices. They are very far away, like perspective in art class. The slippery floor is vanishing up to them and, at the same time, it's all coming closer.

Now we're leaning out of the door to Room 109. I can see Mr. Bender. He's arguing with all these photographers who keep circling around like bad birds. They have cameras that flash little suns in your eyes and they keep poking them at some people Mr. Bender is holding out his arms in front of. I see a tired lady with her arm around her son's shoulder: the TV—the AIDS boy.

They are passing the science room, then the French room. The mother smiles and says to the boy, "Look, you can take French this year."

"Gentlemen, please! This is just what we hoped to avoid by keeping the name of the school secret. You had ample photo opportunities on the school steps. Please, if you'd just let us go about our business. I'm sure there are more newsworthy events happening in our city than this. Gentlemen, *please!*"

121

They are opposite us now. He looks like Toby from Green Knowe, except this boy has brown, too-calm eyes. He's almost smiling. Doesn't he know? "Yes," his eyes are saying, "I know." They've gone by our room. I turn and see Raymond's face, white-angry in back.

"Oh God!" Lisa says. "What are we gonna do now?"

"We're going to cafeteria because it's eleven-thirty," I say. Somehow, we get downstairs, following the steam from the drowned hot dogs through the double cafeteria doors. It's thunderingly silent in there. I mean, it's full of kids, but there's only *one* kid. He's at a table by himself, except for three or four teachers who keep fussing around him. They're talking "nice" to him, you can tell. And he's looking at his tray with the little departments for the fried chicken, the glop of mashed potatoes, and the little paper cup of canned fruit salad, but he's not touching it.

Jennifer, LaTanya, Rohina, and Tiffany Kim are at our table. Rohina and Tiffany are grabbing their lunch bags against their chests like it's a protection. Jennifer and LaTanya are not talking a word. Everybody's just staring at *him*. When I sit down, Jennifer suddenly says, "Laura, he's so cute. How could he have AIDS?" And Tiffany asks me, "Why are there police? Is it a crime?"

"If he gits everybody else sick, they oughta put him in jail," LaTanya says.

"But his mother hasn't gotten sick and she hugs him and everything," I tell them.

"Don't you think it takes courage, a person going

122

where he's not wanted, just because he has the right to go there?" Grampa is saying to me. And I'm talking in my mind to that boy: "Don't die. Stay alive as long as you can, and come to school."

"Where you goin', Laura? Laura!"

"Err, mind if I sit down?" I put my lunch on the table and take a seat. "The food isn't always this bad. But you could bring your own lunch. Some kids do, for instance, me." I'm running out of things to say when Krystal sits down across from us with her bag of chips and a can of soda. "How ya doin?" she says to him. It's like nothing is happening and she's relaxing in Africa.

Then Hector wanders over and sticks out his hand. "Hector's yuh man." And the boy shakes it. "Tim," he says, smiling this serious way he has.

"Yeah, Tim. Well, Tim, stay cool wit' a smile, 'at's duh style. I gotta go pick up my deli order. See ya aroun'." And Hector heads for the side door where a small kid delivers his pizza or pastrami sandwich to him every day.

"I don't know how they can make the chicken so decrepitated," I say.

He picks up this dry, skinny wing. "Should I risk my life?" He's got a *really* good sense of humor!

"What language are you taking?" I'm thinking what his mother said when they went by the French room.

"Well, I'd like to take a couple—maybe French and Spanish."

"In this junior high you only get to take one, French, but in high school and college, there's lots you can pick."

123

Oh no! That was dumb! He might not be here for high school and college. I look to see if he's thinking that, but he says, "I know the college I want to go to but you have to be *really* good to get in, and I'm a goof-off sometimes." He grins and I do too.

"You'll like it here. It's a pretty excellent school," I tell him.

By now the usual cafeteria noise-mess is going on all around, but some kids are still looking like this table is full of criminals and maniacs. For the rest of the time we don't say much, but he's eating at least.

After lunch, Martha squeals up to me in the hall, "Laura! I heard you sat right next to him! What's he like? Ooh, Laura, you're so courage-us!"

"He's funny, and nice. He's just like anybody." I think, *that* couldn't have really been courage. I didn't knock anybody out of the way of a truck, or beat the Nazis or anything.

"Oh God, Laura! Wasn' ya scared?" Lisa and Denise ask me from about fifteen feet away. It wasn't scary. It was—peaceful, somehow. "Don' come near, please, Laura!" they scream. But I don't care.

Mom and Dad jump up. They were waiting on the couch. I never saw them home at 3:30 in the afternoon, but they closed the restaurant when a customer said he saw Junior High 212 on TV.

"Laura, darling! He's not in your class, is he?"

"No, Mom, he's not."

"Thank God! Listen, Laura, we know you—with your sick kittens, little birds with a broken neck. Under *no* circumstances, in *no* conditions will I allow you to go near that boy! Maybe we should put

124

her in a private school, Leonard? In private school they don't have AIDS children next to a well child."

"Mom, I don't *want* to go to private school."

"How do you know what you want? How do you know what's safe, what's not safe? You're only twelve years old—"

"I'll be thirteen tomorrow."

"It takes *much* older than thirteen to know what's good for you."

"Sarah, calm down. You're getting hysterical."

"Oh, now I'm hysterical because I want to save my only child!" And she's sobbing into a Kleenex.

Dad tries to say something, but she's like a car without any brakes. She can't stop. "Laura, Dad and me, we're not getting any younger, you know. And you being an only child, it wouldn't hurt you to do what we *beg* you. *Please,* darling! Don't go near that boy!"

"Mom, *please!* Relax, don't feel so bad. Nothing is going to happen. I'm very healthy, thanks to you. I'll be all right, I promise."

The phone rings. It's Aunt Gertrude. She saw the television too. I close my door, but I can still hear them.

"Gertrude, I can't talk now. I'm too upset. Yes, she's all right. I'll call you back."

"I don't know if you should have said like that to her," Dad says. "It's her birthday tomorrow, and maybe we're spoiling it."

"What do you mean? Of course, I should say! She's a child and children don't know anything about what's life, what's death. That's why we're the parents. Of course I should say it. Don't be foolish, Leonard. Listen to what I'm telling you."

FOURTEEN

It's my own birthday and I wish I didn't have to go to it. If only Mom and Dad didn't make these plans to take me to a restaurant for my thirteenth birthday.

Daddy said, "What would you say if I tell you we are taking you out to a *real* restaurant for your first teenage birthday? A present, of course, you'll get too."

I told him, "I don't need a present, too, Daddy. And the S & L *is* a real restaurant. Nobody could beat your potato pancakes or Mom's raisin strudel."

"The world is not only raisin strudel and potato *latkes*, Laura. There is the French type of cooking, and the Greek, and Italian, and who knows what else? We'll go uptown and sit down like regular people. We'll be the customers this time. After all, we have to celebrate your thirteenth birthday with a smash."

So, Mom is getting all dolled up—that's what she calls it when ladies put on their high heels and Control-Top Panty Hose and fix their hair in rollers to go out someplace. She's taking out the rollers at her vanity table. I gaze into the mirror, expecting to see a monster who is going to make her only parents not live as long as they should, due to aggravation and worry from their daughter!

"Laura, should I put on these earrings? Or, maybe no earrings because it might be too much, with this pin and bracelet and necklace set?"

"I think the earrings would be good *with* the pin and bracelet and necklace set."

"You do?"

"Yep, I do."

"All right. I'll take your word for it." And Mom stands up, looking so different from in the S & L! She's sort of embarrassed to look so nice.

Daddy has on his blue suit, a perfectly white shirt with a stiff collar in two little V's, a wide, shiny yellow tie we gave him for Father's Day. It looks a little big on him, like the gangster in *Scarface Woman*, but he says he loves it. "That's the new style this year, wide."

"Can I have a date with you, Miss Warmbrand?" (That's Mom's name before she was married.) "And with you also, Miss Fine, our birthday girl?" Daddy puts out one elbow for Mom and one for me, and out the door we go, like in a Gene Kelly movie.

I love it when Daddy does funny things like that, but today it only makes it worse. We're all pretending yesterday didn't happen.

Now we're crossing over the other way at night on the Queensboro Bridge, and going straight across Second Avenue, not left to downtown. Grampa isn't with us, because he likes to stay in his house on the

Lower East Side and go to bed early. We'll have our private party later, just Grampa and me.

My shirtwaist dress is nice, that is, pretty nice. Lisa and Denise would say, "Oh God!" But at least it's pink. Mom likes it because it's dressy, but not too dressy, so you can wear it for different purposes like the dance and a restaurant. My tiny gold locket on a chain makes me feel special, the way you want to feel when you are going to a real uptown restaurant. Only it's all spoiled—

I want to yell, "It's too late! I did it already!"

We are going to Mama Lucia's Italian Grotto on 53rd Street.

"Leonard, what do you think we should order? I hope it wouldn't be too expensive there. You can get terrible indigestion from Italian food if you're not accustomed."

"Look at her! We didn't even get there yet and already she's worried! Tell her, Laura, tell her she should relax and enjoy."

"You should, Mom. Probably you could order pizza or spaghetti with meatballs. You have Pepto-Bismol tablets in your purse if you need them."

"Not spaghetti with meatballs! Something different, more unusual," Daddy says.

"Look out! Leonard, that truck came so close! What kind of a driver is that? We'll be lucky if we're alive when we get to Mama Lucia's Italian—what was that, Laura?"

"Grotto, Mom. It means 'cave.' I looked it up. It said, 'An artificial recess made to resemble a natural cave.'"

"Sarah, if you don't relax, you won't be able to

128

enjoy your dinner. 'Sit back and leave the driving to me.' You know who says that, Laura? The Greyhound Bus people. That's their motto."

When we've finally found a parking garage on the West Side that isn't ten dollars for the first half hour, we are ready for the restaurant. A doorman in a green coat with gold buttons holds the door open for Mom and me, but Daddy rushes through first, looking all around, I think, to be sure it's really a nice enough restaurant for his wife and daughter.

Inside, we have to get used to the only light being little lamps with fishnets on them at each table. We can see rough, blue walls with fishnets drooped on them to represent a cave.

"This is beautiful, so attractive!" Mom whispers to Daddy and me.

"It is, Daddy!"

A busy man with a black suit and a little black tie in a bow, tapping a menu against his hand, comes to take us to a table in the back. "Not too much in back," Daddy tells him, but I say when we are sitting down, "It's more like a grotto here than in front."

Nobody is staring at us, still I feel we're different somehow from the other people in this big cave-room. In fact, nobody is even looking at us at all. They are talking and laughing quietly to each other, and they don't even look up at him or say anything when the waiter puts their dish down in front of them. Imagine that happening with Ellen at the S & L!

Here is our waiter, sliding a huge menu book in front of each of us. Daddy sits up holding it wide open and says, "What would you like to have, ladies?"

"It's all in Italian," Mom whispers to him.

"Of course! Why not! What did you expect? This is an Italian restaurant. Pick out something and we'll order it. It certainly sounds like it's delicious, everything in here."

I smile up at the waiter. Maybe he will help us decide? He is looking past me with his hands behind his back. We have *got* to have a good time. They deserve to have a good time. I mean, they planned this for me to be happy.

"What's tasty today?" Daddy asks cheerfully.

"The *polpo con salsa* is excellent, sir."

"Would you like that, Momma? Uh, what is exactly *polpo con salsa?*"

"That is octopus in sauce, sir."

"Oh no, Leonard!" Mom is scared as if the waiter might try to make her eat that.

"I tell you what," Daddy tells the waiter. "Bring us the dinner. Minestrone soup—that's like your vegetable soup," he tells Mom, "and yes, spaghetti with meatballs. Also, two beers, and what would you like, Laura? A Pepsi?" I nod.

"Imported or domestic beer, sir?"

"Budweiser is good, or Miller if you have it."

We're all relieved when he goes away. But I don't want Dad or Mom to feel that I'm disappointed, so I show them the painted pictures on the walls of old-fashioned Italian men in short pants and ladies with kerchiefs dancing at a picnic. The picnic is by a blue bay with a volcano.

Mom says, "Maybe they're eating octopus in sauce, and that's why they're jumping all around."

When the soup comes, I tell her, "It's not nearly

as good as yours, Mom." But it's very tasteful. In fact, I pull it in with a long sipping sound so the waiter can tell the cook we are enjoying it, like Daddy's customers do. It gets very quiet—the only noise is me alone, eating my soup. My face turns a shameful red, and I put down my spoon.

Luckily, the waiter flies a giant plate of spaghetti over our heads and down in the center of the table. With two long spoons he mixes it and flips it on our plates quick like a magician, but he's really bored.

"Ha! This looks good," says Daddy, and he tucks in his napkin under his collar. "Have to save my Father's Day tie from any spots." Nobody in this grotto has a napkin under their chin. I immediately tuck mine in too. Mom spreads hers on her lap, and nervously begins to stir the spaghetti and poke at it. "You have to try different things, Sarah. It makes life much more interesting." Daddy is eating with a good appetite.

The sauce is from the volcano! I mean it is like fiery red lava with soft rocks in it, the rocks being the meatballs. It's good, but it's *too* interesting. Gramma used to make white spaghetti with butter and ketchup on it for my lunch. Anyway, the bread is pully and crunchy. You can eat as much as you want from the little basket. Funny, the other people look like they are in a movie of people eating in a restaurant. Nobody looks like moms or dads. We are the only regular family from Queens here, I guess.

Here comes our snobby waiter with a rolling cart three layers high. It has castles of chocolate devil's food twirled with white icing towers, and little open pies with the gold and red and green fruit looking as if it's painted in a picture, and gushing mountains of whip cream on top of giant red strawberries.

"Do we get some of all these desserts?" I almost say "Goody!" like a little kid. The waiter looks painful and bored. Mom and Dad laugh and they say, "No, Laura. This restaurant would go out of business if they gave so much desserts with the dinner."

Finally, I pick something that looks like a hot dog roll with yellow custard cream oozing out and a long, shiny lick of chocolate over the top. "Ah, the young lady wishes an eclair," says the waiter, pinching it with pinchers and swinging it onto my plate.

Mom and Dad have cheesecake. "Such a stingy piece I would never give," she whispers when it comes. But it turns out it's very rich, so it's all right. "Leonard, do you remember Aunt Gussie's cheesecake?"

"Do I remember? Of course, I remember. If it wasn't for Aunt Gussie's cheesecake, there wouldn't be a Laura."

"Leonard, look out what you're saying to the child."

"Listen, Laura—when your mom and I were supposed to get married, the bakery made a mistake. And our wedding cake with the little groom and bride on top went to somebody else's wedding. So Momma said, 'Without a cake I'm not getting married.' And did she cry!"

"Oh Leonard, I didn't say it like that—"

"So, Aunt Gussie had a cheesecake she made for something else, I forget what, and she cut it up so it could be one piece on top of a bigger piece, and they put the little dolls on top, and we got married. Did we ever tell you that story before, Laura?"

"Maybe Gramma did, but I like to hear you tell it."

"Maybe your mother didn't tell you because she was ashamed she made such a fuss."

"I thought I told you already, Laura. Besides, who wouldn't make a fuss when it's their only wedding in their whole life? You'll see, Laura, when it comes time for your wedding."

"Laura a thirteen-year-old. *Our* Laura, a teenager. I can't believe it," Dad says.

"Mom and Dad, I've *got* to tell you something. It's too late! I don't want to give you worry, but I already did it! And I don't really think I'm bad, because there *is* the First Amendment, you know."

"You went to that boy. I *knew* it. In my heart, I knew it." Mom grabs her chest.

"But the First Amendment says you can have free speech, even if the king is against you. You can have your own thoughts and believe what you really believe, maybe even if it's against your own parents. And you are terribly good parents! Ever since I've been alive, I've always loved you.

"But I couldn't help it. Krystal said, 'Supposin' it was *you*?' I mean, supposing it *was* me, Mom? Supposing I had AIDS!" I burst into tears. Mom bursts into tears.

"Sarah, *shhh*, please! The whole grotto is looking at you!"

"But what if the doctors are wrong? Even the professors are sometimes wrong. Maybe you *could* catch it by being next to somebody?"

"Sarah, they already proved it a thousand times—"

Mom is twisting up her napkin. "What can I say?

133

I can't say that people should scream at *my* child, 'Get away!' like she was something dirty. What can I say?"

"So, you can say, 'Laura, be happy on your thirteenth birthday!' Ladies, I want to make a toast—all raise their glasses! First, the regular Jewish toast, *'La Chayim!* To life!' Come on, Sarah!

"Next, to our dear, dear Laura, and the First Amendment! You have to clink the glasses, Sarah, everybody together!"

Mom sniffles a while, then she clinks, "To our dear, darling Laura—*and* her First Amendment."

The snooty-penguin waiter is looking like he swallowed an iceberg, but we don't care! We're the Fine family, from Queens, New York!

About the Author

MIRIAM COHEN's first novel, *Born to Dance Samba*, was a *Parents' Choice* award book of 1985, and was featured on "Good Morning, America." *The Horn Book* said of her second novel, *Robert and Dawn Marie 4ever,* "Quite simply a lovely story, romantic and optimistic . . . The novel is as fresh and innocent as spring."

Mother of three grown sons, Miriam Cohen has written eighteen books for children. She lives in Queens, New York (like Laura Leonora), with her husband, a professor and painter.